P9-EMK-208

Faith Wish

Other books by James Bennett

A Quiet Desperation

I Can Hear the Mourning Dove

Dakota Dream

The Squared Circle

The Flex of the Thumb

Blue Star Rapture

Plunking Reggie Jackson

Old Hoss (*written with Don Raycraft*)

Faith Wish

+

JAMES BENNETT

Holiday House / New York

To the memory of
Robert Bruce Earle,
dearest friend
and soul mate
J. B.

Printed in the United States of America
www.holidayhouse.com
First Edition

Library of Congress Cataloging-in-Publication Data
Bennett, James W., 1942–
Faith Wish / James W. Bennett.—1st ed.
p. cm.
Summary: Upset with the course her life has taken, pretty and popular senior Anne-Marie is drawn to the leader of a cult-like Christian group, becomes pregnant, and runs away to figure out what the Lord wants her to do with her life.
ISBN 0-8234-1778-6 (hardcover)
[1. Cults—Fiction. 2. Christian life—Fiction. 3. Pregnancy—Fiction. 4. Sisters—Fiction.] I. Title.

PZ7.B43989 Fai 2003
[Fic]—dc21 2002027470

Contents

March 26

Right after pizza, which was served in the church basement, they went to tabernacle.

It wasn't the youth group from Anne-Marie's church; she was only going for the ride because Brooke Sanchez, her best friend, had invited her.

Anne-Marie couldn't get up much enthusiasm for an evening of hellfire-and-brimstone preaching. For that matter, neither could Brooke. But as Brooke had insisted earlier in the day, it was *strategy.*

As soon as the pizza boxes were disposed of and the tables washed, they piled into three cars. Anne-Marie sat next to Brooke in the backseat of a large Buick, driven by a sponsor whose name was Mrs. Strunk. She'd asked them if they all had money for the collection plate. Anne-Marie only had a twenty-dollar bill; it would be gauche to make change from the collection plate. But it would be just as gauche, or maybe even more so, if you put nothing in.

Whatever enthusiasm Anne-Marie and Brooke lacked for

the event was more than made up for by the other passengers. They were already asking who the evangelist was going to be.

"It's Brother Jackson, from Oklahoma," said Mrs. Strunk.

"Oh, I heard him once in Des Moines," said Sara Curtis. "He's been baptized in the Spirit; sometimes he even speaks in tongues!"

"Is he going to speak in tongues?" asked Coleen Hoose.

"No one can predict that," Sara replied. "He can only wait upon the Spirit, like anybody else."

"Is he like, real spiritual?" asked Coleen.

"He's way spiritual," Sara confirmed. "Spiritual and bold."

Anne-Marie looked at the back of their heads. She knew them from school, but not well. Sara and Coleen were both in the National Honor Society, but they were dorks all the same. The two girls were founding members of a Christian Right group that had started a prayer-around-the-flagpole scene, where everybody held hands in a circle and prayed in the parking lot with their eyes squeezed shut.

The tabernacle grounds were on the other side of the Fox River, by a forest preserve beyond the fairgrounds. The drive would take half an hour, at least. *What am I doing here?* Anne-Marie asked herself.

"I only want to go because Chris Weems goes," Brooke had confessed immediately after school.

"What difference does it make if I go, then?"

"It's just for support, okay? Aren't we best friends?"

Anne-Marie didn't think Chris Weems was all that cool anyway. "He's a pretty boy who never gets into trouble. That's about it. You can see him at school," she'd pointed out.

"Yeah, but I think this might be a way to make a good impression," Brooke had responded. "He's like real religious. And he's more than a pretty boy, Anne-Marie. He's a candidate for valedictorian and he's into the drama club big-time."

"Oh. Good for him."

"It's called strategy, Anne-Marie."

"If what you want is strategy, why don't you join the drama club? You can still try out for the spring one-acts. I hear Chris is even writing one of them."

"I don't have the time," Brooke had replied. "I've got cheerleading and orchestra."

"Why don't you come early in the morning for the prayer circle around the flagpole? You could even hold hands with him."

"Get real."

"Why don't you just become a nun? Then he'd *really* be impressed."

"Shut up. Like I'd be a good fit with nuns."

Anne-Marie had giggled before saying, "I guess there's no hope, then. You're too sinful for Chris Weems."

"Oh, and you're Snow White, huh?"

"No, but I'm not pretending to be, just to impress somebody."

"I still think he could be pretty cool." Before she had

exited the parking lot, Brooke lit up. Then she offered a cigarette to Anne-Marie.

"No thanks."

"What, are you quitting?"

"I already quit. Two weeks ago. You should, too. You'll never impress people like Chris Weems if you're a smoker."

"Duh."

"It shows how evil you are."

Brooke had laughed before answering. "Well, I'm not going to smoke when I go to their meetings. I'm not stupid, okay?"

The sun was setting by the time Mrs. Strunk eased the Buick into the narrow lane at the entrance to the forest preserve. Already, there were dozens of cars parked on the gravel shoulders. The girls had to walk several hundred yards on an uneven blacktop to get to the tabernacle, which rose in a near valley. The building was large, but didn't look religious. It was nothing more than a large shelter without walls. Steel poles held up its roof.

On the way, Anne-Marie got separated from Brooke, who was staying as close as possible to Chris Weems. There were so many people here. There were black people. There were trailer-trash whites—men with beer bellies and Harley belt buckles and muscle shirts and too many tattoos. There were Hispanic men in cowboy hats and boots. In short, not the kind of people who would ever show up in Anne-Marie's own comfy-cozy Presbyterian church.

She found herself being swept along between Sara and

Coleen. The surge of people hemmed her in; *I can't stop or turn around.* She shared the alarm of the Canada geese, fleeing and honking as if these holy hordes were unwelcome invaders.

"Are you okay?" Sara asked.

"What?"

"I said, are you okay? You look so pale."

"I'm a little afraid," Anne-Marie told her. "Maybe it's the geese."

Sara was more annoying than Coleen because she always needed to touch. She hooked Anne-Marie's arm and patted her shoulder. "Are you afraid of geese?"

"No, it's just that I'm supposed to write a term paper about them and I know I won't get it done on time."

"Don't think about school right now," said Sara. "Think about the Lord and how He might bless you tonight."

Anne-Marie knew it wasn't the geese anyway, even though she was telling the truth about the term paper. The size of the crowd kept growing as they neared the tabernacle. *I don't have any control here. That's why I'm afraid.* The swollen masses flowed like current, and there was nothing to do but give in to it, just go with the flow. Yet her surrender didn't erase her disorientation. In fact, it brought some panic with it. *Can I be grateful for Sara's arm!?* She gripped it tighter as they moved.

Anne-Marie felt relieved when they reached the shelter; she could lean against one of the poles and take a few deep breaths. *Why am I scared?* Her reaction surprised her. *I've been in crowd flow like this lots of times at concerts and games.*

It was standing room only in the shelter, where the tabernacle service was beginning. There must have been more than 400 people singing a hymn of praise. With robust voices, they split the evening sky like a high school crowd cheering a slam dunk. After a deep breath, Anne-Marie thought: *This is totally trippy, but I've never felt it before. That's why I'm afraid. I don't have an anchor here.*

The shining faces, aglow with joy and passion, didn't look trashy anymore. Some people were waving their arms above their heads. Already unsteady, Anne-Marie stood timidly at the edge of the shelter. Long, crude wooden benches offered the only seating. There were no empty seats nearby. *I'm glad,* she thought. *I need to be on the edge. I need to know I can escape or go my own way if I want.* Sara and she leaned against one of the steel support poles, still holding hands. *I hate holding hands,* she reminded herself. *Especially with touchy-feely people like Sara Curtis.* But at this point in time, at this moment, she needed it.

The noise level was practically deafening, louder and louder with each passing verse of the unfamiliar hymn:

Ride on, ride on, in majesty!
Hark! all the tribes hosanna cry,
O Savior meek, pursue Thy road
With palms and scattered garments strowed!
Ride on, ride on, in majesty!
The wingèd squadrons of the sky
Look down with sad and wondering eyes
To see the approaching sacrifice.

There were no musical instruments, not even a piano. The crescendoing, bold singing voices didn't need any. The elevating gusto caught Anne-Marie off guard; with no warning, she felt lifted up to a high place, her fear dissipating. Now she wasn't moving; the current wasn't a river flow, but voltage. The congregation's zeal, the closed eyes in uplifted, shining faces, the arms swaying back and forth, generated electrical current.

But the change in Anne-Marie's spirit was so rapid and unexpected that it disoriented her. *What am I doing here?* she asked herself. *What is happening here?*

Ride on, ride on, in majesty!
In lowly pomp ride on to die;
Bow Thy meek head to mortal pain.
Then take, O Christ, Thy power and reign.

The sudden silence that followed the singing intensified the charged atmosphere, cutting her loose from all things familiar. A foreign but irresistible magnet drew her into the electric field. *Now I'm an electron. Whose orbit am I in?*

"What?" asked Sara, in a whisper.

"Nothing."

"Are you okay?"

"I don't know what I am. I don't know myself." She trembled, shivered. Why would she be cold wearing a school letter jacket?

"Give in to it," Sara urged in a louder whisper. "Go where the Lord would take you."

Anne-Marie couldn't answer. Still trembling slightly, she was thankful when a small space at the end of a nearby bench opened up enough room for the two of them, if they squeezed together tight. It comforted Anne-Marie that they were sitting at the edge of the building; she could look out into the night sky as the maples and pin oaks faded from view, as the first stars formed. It was warm for March, but the maple branches were still bare and stark against the purple-rose sunset.

Their broken silhouettes reflected the helter-skelter grabbing at her stomach and her heart. The fear, panic, comfort, apprehension, mystery, and voltage fought to claim her core, but merely tumbled one on top of the other, only to recede and swell rapidly from moment to moment.

She turned back to Sara, who was still gripping her right hand while praying in a whisper Anne-Marie couldn't hear. The silence had changed to a low humming. People throughout the tabernacle began to pray, muttering, mumbling, and whispering. She repeated her own thoughts in a whisper that trembled: *What is happening here? Shall I pray now?* She felt like she could. *Shall I say, the Lord is my shepherd . . .* but then she realized, *that's a psalm, not a prayer. But maybe a psalm was a prayer, what else could it be?*

"Brother Jackson is coming," Sara whispered to Anne-Marie.

"How do you know?"

"I saw him behind the curtain. He's getting ready to

come out." She squeezed Anne-Marie's hand again before she said, "You're not still afraid, are you?"

Anne-Marie swallowed hard. "Yes and no . . . I can't say for sure. . . . No." The lump in her throat brought her up short, but it was the truth. Little by little her fear moved aside to make room for the mystery of anticipation. "I'm just mixed up," she finally added.

Then Sara took her arm again, as well as her hand. "It's the Lord's challenge, Anne-Marie. His invitation. Let Him into your life."

There wasn't time to answer: Brother Jackson came on stage and she was locked on him in spite of herself. He was beautiful, nothing like what she expected. He stared boldly at the crowd for a full minute, or even longer, without speaking, standing with his hands on his hips, his dark eyes traveling slowly from face to face. If he had even a trace of self-consciousness or nerves, Anne-Marie couldn't detect it. The longer his eyes traveled from one person to the next, the more she felt the lump in her throat.

She sucked in her breath sharply when the eyes fastened on her own; now she had goose bumps to go with her chills. It was as if by simply looking into eyes he could craft a spiritual bond that no words could name. The hush had become so complete it was palpable; the honking of a single goose seemed as loud as a public-address system.

It was then that Brother Jackson spoke: "How 'bout Jesus tonight?"

His question seemed to break the spell. No one spoke, but there was scattered applause.

Brother Jackson smiled with peaceful assurance, then he asked another question: "Who loves you?"

A few voices answered, "Jesus," but somewhat timidly and not immediately. Brother Jackson cocked his hand next to his ear before he repeated his question. "*Who* is it loves you?"

"Jesus!" proclaimed the throng, this time without hesitation.

Then, practically shouting, he said, "Say what? Now one more time, tell me who it is that loves you!"

"JESUS!" This time it was as loud as a crowd galvanized by a game-winning touchdown. Anne-Marie felt chills again, this time up and down her spine, and they had nothing to do with the cool night air. She zipped her letter jacket up snug around her neck.

"Then how 'bout Jesus every night?" the evangelist asked with a smile.

Anne-Marie heard the murmured responses, but she couldn't help staring at Brother Jackson. He was lean, but the definition of his muscles was sharp. The sleeves of his blue work shirt were rolled up high enough to reveal his biceps. He looked really strong, as blessed in his body as in his soul. There was a greenish tattoo on his right forearm, but Anne-Marie wasn't close enough to make out what it was. His lustrous, dark hair was pulled back into a modest ponytail. The track lights above the stage seemed to highlight his even suntan; she guessed he must have just arrived from a preaching mission somewhere in the South.

But most of all, it was his smile. Radiant and captivating, it seemed to flash across his face with each right answer like heat lightning. He didn't *preach.* He would ask and they would answer. "*When* does He love you?"

"All the time," answered someone promptly.

"*All* the time!"

"Come on, do come on."

"When you're good?" asked Brother Jackson.

"Come on."

"Yes!"

"Lord yes!" declared the fellowship of believers.

"When you're bad?"

"Yes!"

"That's right."

"When you sin?"

"Yes!"

He will ask and we will know, thought Anne-Marie. *It's not in the knowing, but the saying. We will know the answers, then will be the giving and taking, back and forth. Each time the voltage will increase; people will be swept along like rafters on a river bound for glory.* She had never known such feelings before. The knot of anticipation in her stomach loosened with the ongoing ebb and flow between Brother Jackson and the flock.

The evangelist spoke more quietly. "When does God turn his back on you?"

"Never."

"Never!" shouted a man near the back.

"Bring it on, that's right," said Sara loudly.

Anne-Marie whispered timidly, "Never."

"How many of you are sinners?" asked Brother Jackson in a more urgent tone.

Every hand went up immediately. Anne-Marie followed the rest.

A tall black man was standing about twenty feet away. "I have sinned against my fellow man!" he declared. "I am powerless against sin, but I know to lay my burdens at the throne."

"Praise God for that testimony," said Brother Jackson, with the magnetic smile once again spreading across his face. "And when does the Lord ignore your cries? When does He hide His face from you?"

"Never!"

"Never," said Anne-Marie quietly.

Brother Jackson directed the congregation as surely as any conductor led an orchestra. The lump in her throat felt nothing like her customary knot of remorse and guilt. The lump was splendid somehow, and the tingling that spread throughout her limbs felt wholly spiritual.

How many times had she heard these themes in church, that God's love was unconditional, that if you confessed, your sins would be forgiven? Hundreds? That the grace of God wasn't a limited-time offer? Hundreds more?

But it was this time, this place, and most of all, this man. That's what was different. She thought of a Bible verse, *He makes all things new,* but wouldn't know where in the Bible to look for it.

Brother Jackson was asking, "Who has a ticket for God's grace?"

"We do!"

"All of us! No one is left out!"

"Come on, *do* come on!"

Anne-Marie had to turn away, her face suddenly wet with tears. Brother Jackson was too glorious to look at. She turned to the woods without seeing the maple limbs. Sara was gripping her right knee tightly when she wasn't waving her arms in the air.

I'm going to be different now, Anne-Marie told herself. *I can surrender.*

She removed Sara's grip from her knee, stood up slowly, and walked toward the woods. She couldn't look at Brother Jackson a moment longer; it was like staring into the sun. Nobody noticed her exit, and she wouldn't have known if they did. She felt a comfort zone, like a spiritual cocoon of the Lord's own making. *I'm going to be different now,* she told herself again.

She shivered, body and soul. When she was close enough to smell the trees, she stood unknowingly in a puddle of water. She promised God she would stop smoking for good and never drink any more beer. Even though she hadn't been intimate with Richard Bone for at least two months, she resolved never to have sex with him again, no matter how persistent he might be. She assured God that she would honor her parents and get her homework done on time, even the term paper.

She spoke out loud: "It's not that I'm *going* to be different, I'm *already* different."

In the distance, she heard a single, muffled honk. A phrase from the unfamiliar hymn, "the wingèd squadrons of the sky," danced in her head. She found herself praying for all the Canada geese, living and dead.

She wiped her tears with tissues before returning to the tabernacle. A closing hymn was in progress, but it, too, was unfamiliar. Why should it matter, though? If it was praising God, did she need to know the words? Brother Jackson was in the bright light. His arms above his head, his eyes closed, he swayed in lofty splendor.

The collection plate, a simple woven basket, came by. Anne-Marie dropped in her twenty-dollar bill without a second thought.

April 10

Anne-Marie sat in front of her computer on an evening so warm and fresh she opened one of her windows. The phone rang.

It was Sara Curtis. "I'm just calling to apologize for not following you to the woods at Brother Jackson's tabernacle meeting."

Sara Curtis rarely called her. "Please don't apologize. I really needed to be alone."

"You needed to pray alone, huh?"

"Yes. That's it."

"Did you feel like the Lord was blessing you, taking you into His arms?"

"Yes, I guess I did."

"Praise God for it," Sara answered immediately. "Do you feel strong in the Fellowship?"

Anne-Marie hesitated for several seconds. "I guess I do, but not enough. I guess I could."

"Just let yourself surrender every day and the Lord will lead you."

Anne-Marie confessed, "I feel different, but the world's the same."

"I know just what you mean," Sara replied immediately. "When I first became a Christian, a real part of the Fellowship, I felt the same way. My pastor explained it to me this way: When you're a born-again Christian, it's as shining as a crystal in the sun, but as fragile as a soap bubble in the wind."

"That's it!" gushed Anne-Marie. "That's it exactly."

"How's the world the same, Anne-Marie?"

Anne-Marie moved to the edge of the bed. She wanted to share her fears and insecurities, and Sara was someone she could trust. "I'm getting two unsatisfactory progress reports, which means I'm probably not on track to graduate on time. My biology research paper is still stuck on square one. All of my friends will be going through the ceremony, but I won't want to be anywhere near."

"The Lord will lead you in your academics too, if you surrender," said Sara. "What's your biology term paper about?"

"Shaking goose eggs."

"Shaking goose eggs? What's that mean?"

"Authorities in the northwest suburbs are trying to cut back on the overpopulation of Canada geese. Their main strategy is the shaking. They chase mothers from their nests, then shake the eggs hard, the way you might shake up a carton of orange juice. When the mother goose returns to the nest, she's sitting on dead eggs, but there's no way for her to know it."

"Yuck. It sounds so sad."

"I know it sounds sad, which is why I'd like to write the paper on it. I just don't follow through on big projects, Sara."

"Take this suffering to the Lord and He will lift you up."

"If you want the truth," Anne-Marie continued, "the idea wasn't really my own. My mother brought me a series of articles she'd saved from the *Tribune*."

"So? It sounds like a good topic to me. What difference does it make where it comes from? You've already made it your own."

"I wish I could say that, but I can't even get a working outline before my concentration runs out."

"Do you believe the Lord can help you?"

"I'd like to believe it. I've been reading and rereading passages of Scripture. I've almost memorized some of them."

"Praise God," said Sara. "But you need to find a balance."

"A balance?"

"Yes. If you're spending so much time reading Scripture that you can't get homework finished, then you'll still be in the same place. You can set aside a few minutes each day for homework. The Lord loves dedication as much as He loves the reading of His Word."

"You seem to understand so much, Sara."

"I've just been in the Fellowship longer, that's all. We have Bible study meetings every Monday night at my house. Some are from the college, but most are from the high school. You know a lot of them. You'd be welcome to join us any time."

Anne-Marie was enthusiastic. "It would probably help me grow in the faith."

Sara laughed. "Not only you, but many others, too."

After they hung up, Anne-Marie went back to the computer. She tried to concentrate on the title spread across her screen:

To Shake or Not to Shake

by

Anne-Marie Morgan

It frustrated her that she couldn't even start an outline. She moved her mouse around, centering the title, changing the font several times, as well as its size. Anne-Marie was embarrassed by her minimal computer knowledge; it was humiliating when your own mother knew more about computers than you did. In most families, it was just the reverse, but Anne-Marie's mother was a software consultant for a high-tech corporation called Gesko.

Anne-Marie knew what she wanted to say in the term paper—some years earlier the Department of Natural Resources had introduced hundreds of Canada geese into the area. In other words, the problem was man-made, and the authorities could look in the mirror to place the blame.

But how could she outline so much material? Restless again, she picked up her Bible, turned to chapter three of

Revelation, and read some verses recommended by Coleen. Verses 15 and 16 seemed particularly bold and fearless: *"I know your works; you are neither cold nor hot. Would that you were cold or hot! So, because you are lukewarm, and neither cold nor hot, I will spew you out of my mouth."*

This was the core of the born-again message. Lukewarm just wouldn't bring God's favor. Anne-Marie closed out of her term paper folder and printed the verses from Revelation. It was passion she wanted—the spiritual kind—so the term paper could wait.

Then her phone rang a second time. It was Brooke. "Guess what?" she said.

"What?"

"Chris Weems is gay!"

"Get out."

"No, I'm serious," Brooke insisted. "He's gay!"

"How do you know?"

"He told me."

"He told you?"

"He told me he's gay. That's why he goes to prayer groups and Bible study all the time."

"But that can't be the only reason," Anne-Marie protested. "He's way spiritual."

"Not the only reason maybe, but it's the main one. That's why he goes to the tabernacle meetings. He thinks it's a terrible sin that he has to be forgiven for."

Anne-Marie looked at the phone, then at the screen,

then back at the phone again. She was holding the just-printed Revelation verses. Homosexuality was a sin, the Bible was clear about that. But she'd never thought about it much. She knew a few homosexuals, in school and out, but she'd never felt the need to judge them. "What does he pray for?" she asked Brooke. "To be forgiven, or to change?"

"I think mostly he prays to be changed. He believes he can never be a true Christian if he's gay. Don't you think the whole thing is pretty trippy?"

Anne-Marie asked, "How gay is he?"

"What's *that* supposed to mean? He's gay. He's a homosexual."

"Yes, but is he way gay, you know, is he like completely gay?"

"I won't even ask what that means," said Brooke. "Are you okay? You wanna go to Sorrel's?"

Anne-Marie wondered herself what she meant about *how gay.* She answered Brooke by saying, "I can't."

"Why not?"

Sorrel's was a downtown bar where you could get served if you looked old for your age. Anne-Marie and Brooke had been there several times before. "I have to work on this term paper for biology."

"You could work on it tomorrow."

"No, I can't," Anne-Marie repeated.

"Wow," Anne-Marie heard Brooke say. "You really took that tabernacle serious, huh?"

Anne-Marie answered cautiously. She wasn't sure how much of *the new* Anne-Marie Brooke would be ready to handle. "I guess I did," she finally replied. "I think I have to."

There was a long silence on both ends of the line before Anne-Marie eventually said, "I guess if Chris Weems is gay, you won't be interested in him anymore, huh?"

"Duh."

It broke the tension. They giggled before hanging up. Anne-Marie turned back to her computer screen, where the same Bible passage was still in the same place, and in the same font.

Anne-Marie's room had been her older sister Eleanor's room, only remodeled and enlarged. What had been a simple twelve-by-sixteen-foot bedroom was now combined with an airy sunporch to form a bright and spacious twenty-by-twenty-four-foot living space. The room was newly painted in robin's egg blue.

But how could any room, remodeled or upgraded or whatever, make her feel better if she might not even graduate with her class? It was *her* computer, but it was perched on *Eleanor's* old desk. From time to time she looked inside the drawers, flipping through Eleanor's old scholarship offers or academic awards or certificates of achievement. National Merit Scholarship notifications. Full academic scholarship offers from around the country. National Honor Society certificates.

Anne-Marie wondered if she should empty the drawers and fill them up with some of her own stuff. If the room itself was hers, then the desk was, too. But what stuff would it be? The letters from the counseling office explaining how she could make up her schoolwork and still be qualified to take finals? Or maybe some of her past letters which delivered suspensions for cutting classes?

Anne-Marie put her chin in her hands. She stared out the huge picture window, but it was too dark to see much of anything other than streetlights.

The remodeled bookcases near the closet were now configured to form an entertainment center, which housed her Aiwa stereo and her Samsung color TV. She could operate them both by remote, from the desk or from her bed.

Suddenly she was restless and irritable. She wanted to smoke, but she'd given up cigarettes. She did like to pick out Bible verses that comforted or inspired her, then print them. She'd choose different fonts and center them on parchment paper. Many of her favorites were from the Psalms:

Blessed is the man who walks not in the counsel of the wicked,
nor stands in the way of sinners,
nor sits in the seats of scoffers;
but his delight is in the law of the Lord,
and on his law he meditates day and night.

The passage reminded her of one of Brother Jackson's strong admonitions, to "Keep company with the sheep and avoid the goats."

Anne-Marie also loved Psalm 9:

I will give thanks to the Lord with my whole heart;
I will tell of all thy wonderful deeds.
I will be glad and exult in thee,
I will sing praise to thy name,
O Most High.
When my enemies turned back,
they stumbled and perished before thee.

In her mind, the passage triggered another of Brother Jackson's urgings, to celebrate the presence of God every day in her life. It also reminded her of the snares and sinkholes the world held for true believers. She flipped pages in the Bible until she found a passage that read:

Because you have kept my word of patient endurance,
I will keep you from the hour of trial which is coming on the whole world.

The knock on the door startled her; it was her father. She told him to come in. Her screen saver was forming a scrim of snowflakes.

"How's the term paper coming?" he wanted to know.

"Pretty slow," she said. "I'm working on it now."

Her father glanced around at all her printed Bible verses before he said, "If you made this much progress on your homework, you'd probably be in good shape."

"I hope the passages will guide me by giving me strength."

Her father sighed. He was a tall, handsome man whose graying temples looked distinguished.

"I've been thinking about changing my topic," Anne-Marie said timidly.

"Changing it to what?"

"To the prayer circle around the flagpole and the law. When they hold hands and pray, Vice Principal Rosario always monitors them with this look on his face. He holds his walkie-talkie. He says his reason for being there is to make sure the prayers don't last past the second bell. But everybody knows he's there because of the lawsuit."

Anne-Marie's father, who was an attorney, dismissed it with a wave of his hand. "The prayer circle is not a school-sponsored event," he said. "The lawsuit won't hold water."

For a moment, it almost seemed like he was actually standing up for her. "Then why do they persecute us?" she asked.

"*Us?* Have you been involved in the circle?"

Anne-Marie looked down. "Not yet. My faith isn't strong enough yet."

His answer was impatient: "It's got nothing to do with persecution, it's *prosecution*, a simple First Amendment legal action. It goes on all over the country. But even your question itself is reason enough for you to think long and hard about the type of religious group you've gotten yourself into. Groups that talk about persecution *want* to be martyrs and victims. That's not healthy."

"We've been through all this. I don't want to go through it again."

"Neither do I," her father assured her. "Anyway, this topic wouldn't work for biology."

"I know." But she felt the need to defend herself and her faith. "If loving the Lord and wanting to serve Him isn't healthy, then I don't know what would be."

"I don't want to argue with you, Anne-Marie. I just wish you'd spend as much time on your research papers as you do printing out Bible passages."

"You've been looking at my Bible."

"I've seen it. I didn't have time to count the turned-down pages. But I did count these twelve Bible verses you've printed out and pinned to your walls. Perhaps I should be grateful that your computer skills are improving."

"All I really know is how to use the word processing program and the printer. If you've been looking through my Bible, though, you're invading my privacy. This room and computer area are mine now."

Her father ignored the mild protest. "But I've also seen your grades in English and biology," he said. "This religious phase you're going through is just another distraction as far as I can tell, which is the last thing you need."

Anne-Marie bristled at the term *religious phase,* but merely said, "I don't want to talk about it anymore. I'll probably say something I'll regret." *I have to forgive,* she reminded herself. *I have to learn forgiveness.*

April 11

The sheep have to be kept apart from the goats.

Anne-Marie heard her mother calling her from the bottom of the stairs, but it wasn't until the third time that she actually woke up. She rolled on her side, burying her head beneath her pillow. Her dream had been about Brother Jackson and his sermon. It had been vivid enough to recall one of his admonitions again: *Keep company with the sheep, those who can help you find paths of righteousness. Avoid the goats; they are the tempters who set the snares.*

Anne-Marie remembered the man as well as the words. She couldn't forget Brother Jackson's smile or the strength of his body. The dream had such a haloed effect she buried her head deeper beneath the pillow to try to preserve it.

It only took a few moments, though, before she was wide awake and headed for the bathroom. Lathering in the shower, she asked herself, *Can I always tell the difference between the sheep and goats? How do you do that?* She thought again of his face, but the tingling was nothing more than the hot water rinsing down her limbs. She wondered if there was a way to turn showers into daily purification rites, like baptism.

Anne-Marie used her white scrunchie to anchor her long blond hair in a ponytail. It wasn't glamorous, but she'd decided it wasn't important anymore to spend the time and money on her hair. She had tons of makeup in her collection, but it too seemed like overkill, now that she was secure in the Lord. She decided to use only a little mascara and just a touch of lipstick.

She stepped on the scale to discover that she had lost six pounds during the past two weeks. The lost pounds didn't matter—her physical beauty was never at issue, it had always been the source of her popularity at school, no matter that her behavior was sometimes risky and her grades low. Her appetite must be off due to the excitement brought about by her conversion. She was high every day.

Even though it was a particularly warm day, she decided not to let the weather dictate clothing. In her closet was her newest purchase, a plum-colored Lycra tank top she'd bought at Von Maur's on sale for $36. She pushed it aside, realizing that the old Anne-Marie would have worn it in a heartbeat. Would have added a provocative pair of shorts to complete the image. And then might have been sent home by Vice Principal Rosario for exposing too much midriff and other flesh.

Instead, she put on her blue jeans and a modest blouse whose hem touched the top of her empty belt loops.

By the time Anne-Marie got to the kitchen, her mother had gone to work, and her father was about to leave as well.

He was trying to straighten the knot in his tie while drinking coffee at the same time. Since he liked to drink his coffee with a cup *and* a saucer, his task was all the harder.

While she was nibbling around the edges of a toasted bagel, but not actually eating much of it, her father said, "Your front fender is primed, and I've found a perfect paint match at Carl's Auto Body."

"I thought it was in the shop for a timing belt or something."

"They replaced the timing belt, but as long as the car was there, I decided it would be good to go ahead and fix that ding in the fender."

"Great," she said, trying to sound as if she really meant it. She'd never had much enthusiasm for her father's hobby of restoring old cars. A car was to drive, as far as she could see. "Is it okay if I drive it?"

"Not quite yet. I've still got the primer covered for protection. I can't afford to get any moisture on it. You can drive the Chevy, though."

Anne-Marie sighed. The Chevy was a green-and-white '57 Bel Air, a real classic. A lot of people thought it was ultra cool, especially the boys at school. "Okay," she said.

"Did you make any progress on the term paper last night?" he asked her.

"Only a little," she lied. *None whatsoever* would have been more truthful.

"You have to stay with it, Anne-Marie. It's important."

She took a deep breath while she watched bagel crumbs tumble to her plate. She was calm. "I'm working on it," she said again. "I know it's important."

Her father dropped the subject to say, "When your car has that new coat of paint, it'll be just like new."

Just like new, she thought. But now she knew that the only *new* that really mattered was her new self in Jesus. *He makes all things new,* the Bible promised. She must have been lost in thought after that, because the next time she looked up, her father had left.

On the way to school, she remembered how big and boxy the old Chevy was; it seemed like she was driving a train. As bad luck would have it, the first person she met in the school parking lot was Richard Bone. Currently her ex-boyfriend, but also one of the snares. One of the goats. She'd had sex with him several times, but no more. She no longer carried condoms in her purse. Although she now needed ways to fend off his groping, he was mostly good-natured about being rebuffed—usually because he was buzzed on marijuana. He tested her faith each time the two of them found themselves alone.

"Wow. How cool is it?" he said, referring to the Chevy.

"Probably not as cool as you think," she replied.

"Bullshit," he said. "This car is prime. It's *ultra* prime."

"If you say so," Anne-Marie replied. She opened the back door to get her books. "But I don't know why you have to say bullshit."

He ignored the reprimand. "What's up with your own car?"

"My dad is painting my front fender. The paint's not dry enough or something."

"He's probably just got the primer on it. So why didn't you drive the Beamer?"

"My dad would never let me drive the Beamer. You know that."

Richard said, "Hey Anne-Marie; you want to mess around?"

It was just like him, coming out of the blue. "Get real."

"No, seriously. We could just skip school and drive out to the lake. Look at the weather; is this a day to waste in classrooms?" He had the silly grin on his face. There was no telling if he was high or not. He often was. What he usually said was *Anne-Marie, please show me your tits.* So this was better.

"I decided not to try out for the play," he informed her. "I'm burned out on theater."

"That's not what I heard," Anne-Marie declared.

"Give some other people a chance; that's the way I see it. What did you hear?"

"I heard Mr. Burns kicked you out because you were smoking pot while you were building sets."

Richard shrugged before he said, "The rumors are rampant, I guess. Either way, it's the same result."

"He could have turned you in, you know. Consider yourself lucky he didn't call the cops."

"Choices, choices, choices, Anne-Marie. Life is all about choosing, huh? Speaking of the lake—"

"Who's speaking of the lake? Not me, that's for sure."

"The Chevy's got that big backseat."

"Oh please. Besides, I'd appreciate it if you didn't like talk to me that way anymore. Backseats are just for extra passengers."

"Oh, I forgot. You found Jesus."

"And I'd appreciate it," she said as politely as she could, "if you didn't talk to me that way, either."

"Well just excuse me all to hell."

"It's been two months since we broke up, Richard. Get used to it."

"But you have cleft my heart in twain."

"Shut *up*."

"Never was pain so sweet as mine that I can ne'er forsake it."

"Stop it!" He *must* be high. Even though he was one of the goats, in some ways she liked him better now that they weren't in a relationship—she could enjoy him more as a friend than as a boyfriend. "Save your Shakespeare for the stage." She put her books into her backpack.

"I've got condoms," he said.

"It doesn't matter," she replied. "It wouldn't please the Lord if I had sex with you." By this time, they were headed toward the building.

"But you want to anyway, is that what you're saying?"

"Part of me does, but that's the part I have to put behind me."

"You're really gone on this religious trip, aren't you?"

"You could put it that way. The real thing is I've found the Lord and want to serve him."

"How about a hand job sometime?"

"Then all I'd be is like a sexual toy to give you pleasure. You can take care of that yourself. You can even find mechanical hand jobs on plenty of Web sites."

"You visit pornographic Web sites?" he asked.

"No. Brooke tells me about them." They fell in with other groups of students approaching the front door.

"Have you ever seen *Jesus of Montreal?*" he asked her.

"What's that?"

"It's a movie."

"No. I've seen Jesus of Nazareth. He's the only one that counts."

"You sound like a programmed windup toy, Anne-Marie. Anyway, in *Jesus of Montreal,* there's this woman who services this priest from time to time. Her friends ask her why. Want to know her answer?" They were waiting in line for their turn to squeeze through the doors. Richard was now concealing a burning joint in his cupped hand.

"Not really," she said.

"Her answer is, 'It gives him so much pleasure and it's such a small sacrifice on my part.'" He dropped the joint and crushed it beneath his shoe.

"That's supposed to impress me? That's just lame."

"No it's not. It's a unique way of looking at it. If Shakespeare were alive today, he'd probably wish he'd thought of it."

"Okay, then you and Shakespeare can think about it. Richard, all I can do is be your friend. If you can't accept that, then I'm sorry." Maybe she didn't like him better this way—it gave him too much leeway to be a smart-ass if he didn't have anything to lose.

"Maybe I can do that; let me think it over. Flexibility has always been one of my strong points." Then he added, "See you round the flagpole, huh?"

"Stop being obnoxious."

Second-hour English class was both a breeze and a relief. Mr. Shamsky got so wrapped up in *Hamlet* that he quoted long passages theatrically, instead of asking any of his hard questions that put people on the spot. Just before the end of the period, though, Anne-Marie got a slip from one of the runners. She read it over twice while Mr. Shamsky explained how *Hamlet* was modernized in the movies by Mel Gibson and Kenneth Branagh. The note was from Vice Principal Rosario and said, "See me sometime soon about make-up work."

When the bell rang, Anne-Marie decided to skip the resource room and go to regular study hall, because she liked the atmosphere better.

She found an empty computer and tried to work. She wrote: "There's a controversy about Canada geese in the northwest suburbs." She stared at the sentence. She changed it:

"There's a controversy about Canada geese in northwest suburbs like Hoffman Estates and Crystal Lake." That was better. It was more specific. Even so, she found herself stumped.

Then Brooke showed up; without a word, she pulled one of the computer chairs over. She read the sentence on the screen. "How's the term paper going?"

"You're looking at it. One sentence."

"This is all you've got?"

"It's all I've got, okay? Isn't that what I said?"

"Sorry. I didn't mean to piss you off."

"It's just . . . it's just . . . I can't seem to get anything going."

"That's called writers' block. Want me to help you?" asked Brooke. "I will if you want."

"No. I have to do this myself."

Brooke said, "I've been reading about the Canada geese thing in the *Sun-Times*. The most disgusting part is the way they go about getting to the nests so they can shake the eggs."

"What's that? What do you mean?"

"I mean the mother geese are nasty about keeping their nests safe. They are even known to attack. That's why park workers and forest officers use metal garbage can lids as shields to keep them away while they invade the nests and shake the eggs."

"But that's disgusting," said Anne-Marie.

"Totally."

"I'm glad you told me though," said Anne-Marie, "because I can use it in my paper."

"Well, that's good then," said Brooke with a laugh. "I guess I helped you after all."

"I guess. But think about this: You know more about my own subject than I do, and I'm supposed to be the one doing research. How am I supposed to feel about that?"

"Don't put yourself down. You'll do fine. It will all work out."

"It will all work out for *you*. Here's how it's all working out for *me*." She showed Brooke the note from Rosario.

Brooke merely shrugged. "So? It doesn't mean you have to go today. It just says sometime soon."

"Maybe I will go today," said Anne-Marie. "It might be better to get it out of the way."

"Up to you." Brooke shrugged again. "It's no big deal."

"Maybe I should just do it now. This is study hall."

"Not now," her friend replied quickly.

"Why not?"

"Because I've got something to tell you. You've got to hear this."

"Tell me what?"

"Chris Weems asked me out."

"He asked you out? But you said he's gay."

"He *is* gay. But he asked me out anyway. Can you believe it? He tells me he's gay, then asks me out."

"Shut up."

"No, for real. He wants to take me out so he can overcome being gay."

"But what does that mean?" Anne-Marie already felt

sorry for Chris Weems, despite the fact she didn't know him very well. It was too fascinating, though; Rosario's note would have to wait.

"He said I was beautiful," Brooke replied.

"Well, you are."

"And the same to you. I only wish I had that bustline of yours. Anyway. He said if he went out with me, he might be like attracted to a girl. Or at least he would have a good chance."

Anne-Marie was still confused. "Did he mean you were supposed to do something about it? Did he mean he wanted to make out?"

"Maybe. I didn't ask. But can you believe it?"

"So what did you tell him?"

Before she answered, Brooke took her small mirror from her purse and began to check her makeup. "I told him maybe," she said.

"Maybe?"

"I told him if he took me to the Billy Joel concert over at Ravinia, I might think about it."

"But why? Why would you want to go out with a guy who's gay?"

"Just for fun, I guess. I mean, in a way it's kind of a hoot, don't you think? Besides, I just love Billy Joel."

"Billy Joel is out of touch," said Anne-Marie.

"Billy Joel is never out of touch," Brooke said. "He writes all of his own songs, arranges them, performs them, and always draws huge crowds even with high-priced tickets. People who are great musicians are never out of touch."

Anne-Marie didn't feel like arguing. She didn't even know what *arranging* a song would involve. Brooke was a violinist, so she had a much stronger grasp of music.

What did seem to matter was the integrity of it. "But that would be like just using him," she said quietly. "Those tickets would be expensive."

"Don't worry about it. He changed his mind. He said he couldn't go to the concert because he had to go to another one of those tabernacle meetings."

"You mean with Brother Jackson?"

"If that's his name. He's moving on to some other place, so Chris says he doesn't want to miss out."

Brother Jackson is moving on? "When is he moving on? Where is he going?"

Brooke shrugged again before she answered. "How would I know? Wow, that guy *really* got to you, huh?" She snapped the mirror back inside her purse.

Anne-Marie felt a sudden nervous stomach at the center of a whirlwind of pressing emotions. If Brother Jackson was leaving, where was he going? When? Was it any of her business? Chris Weems was gay. That was a sin, pure and simple. Still, you were supposed to love the sinner at the same time you hated the sin.

"I think he's real spiritual," she finally said to Brooke.

"Whatever."

*　　*　　*

Agitation plagued Anne-Marie all the way to the counseling center. She was supposed to be headed to biology, but a sudden burst of guilt and apprehension about her term paper stopped her.

The counseling center had a large waiting room outside the actual offices. Anne-Marie took a seat at one of the round tables. At the next table a couple of boys wearing Sacramento Kings athletic jerseys were seated. One of them was Marcus Toney, a basketball star. Wearing their Kings caps backward, they sprawled in their chairs, laughing and talking. *How could they be so insolent?* Anne-Marie wondered. They could be given detentions or even suspensions within the next few minutes. *Don't they know where they are?* And yet, a part of her admired their indifference.

While she waited, she found her mind wandering into the past, landing on a stinging memory that took her back to October, when she and her parents met with Mrs. DeShields. Anne-Marie had expected the garden-variety pep talk about organizing study time more effectively, but Mrs. DeShields had dropped a bomb: "I'd like to test Anne-Marie for attention deficit disorder," she said.

For some moments, Anne-Marie and her parents were speechless. "Attention deficit disorder?" her mother had finally responded. "I don't understand."

"I believe a good deal of Anne-Marie's academic difficulties may have something to do with a learning disability. I don't think we're talking here about a lazy student who simply won't apply herself. She and I have talked a number of times about her distractibility and inability to focus when she does her schoolwork."

"A learning disability?" Her father had immediately dismissed the entire notion. "Are you trying to tell us our daughter ought to be in special education?"

Anne-Marie had been horrified enough to echo her father's words: "You want me in special ed?"

"No, not exactly," the counselor had replied.

"You want me in LD/BD classes?" The idea was simply mortifying.

"No, not exactly, I said. But I would like to test you for ADD to see if it may be a factor in the academic underachievement that seems to be your pattern."

Her father had leaned forward in his chair with his hands on his knees. "This is crazy. Anne-Marie is a college-bound young woman. And in the middle of her senior year in high school, you're trying to tell us she's learning disabled?"

Then her mother joined the conversation. "What is attention deficit disorder? Even though I've heard a lot about it, I'm not sure I understand what it is exactly."

"It's an inability to focus," Mrs. DeShields had replied. "Or maybe better said, it's the inability to maintain focus. People with ADD don't seem to be able to get on task or stay on task. They can't sequence. Their distractibility and restlessness undercut their ability to stay connected with projects. Particularly academic projects. They seem to return to the same material again and again without moving ahead productively."

Anne-Marie had wanted the conversation to end right then and there. But her mother wanted more information: "If Anne-Marie has this learning disorder, why are we finding out about it now? She's already seventeen years old!"

"We may not be *finding out* anything," the counselor had replied. "That's why I'd like to test her. As for your question, all I can tell you is that the system is not perfect. Special needs students aren't always identified by the ongoing testing that students participate in. Sometimes people slip through the cracks."

"Are you telling me," her father had demanded in his stern cross-examination tone, "that our daughter may have had an undiagnosed learning disorder all these years?"

"I'm telling you it's possible."

"And that could happen after twelve years in school, twelve years of achievement tests, aptitude tests, and all the other standardized testing that students go through?"

Mrs. DeShields had simply repeated herself by saying, "Yes. It's possible. As much as we test, our systems aren't perfect."

Her father had kept boring in: "If the school systems' assessment patterns could be that incompetent, what would be the purpose of another standardized test at this point? Is there any reason to believe this one would be more accurate or useful?"

Anne-Marie had relished her father's aggressive manner—it felt like he was standing up for her in court. "I'll tell you one thing," she'd said. "I'm not going to spend my time coming and going to classes in the west wing. Everybody knows what goes on down there." She almost used the word *retard,* but caught herself just in time.

Mrs. DeShields had been patient. "If that's the way you feel then, we can simply drop the subject. There's nothing that mandates testing a high school senior."

But, characteristically, it was Anne-Marie's mother who had been more open-minded. "What would the test entail?"

"It's simply a four-page standardized test that can be taken in an hour." Mrs. DeShields had smiled and said to Anne-Marie, "I can assure you it would be painless. It's not an invasive procedure."

"Then what would be the point of not taking it?" her mother had wondered out loud.

"The point," Anne-Marie had said immediately, "is that I'd be taking classes in that . . . that *wing. I'm* the one who would have to suffer all the embarrassment."

"Not necessarily," the counselor replied quickly. "For all we know, the test will show that you're not ADD. And even if you are, I would only suggest one change in your course schedule. Instead of taking your regular study hall, you would be taking it in the resource room."

"What the hell is the resource room?" her father had demanded, still twisting in his chair uncomfortably.

"It's an organized study hall," was Mrs. DeShields's answer. "Mrs. Quinn is the teacher. She works with students individually on organizing their homework, checking assignment deadlines and work sheets, helping with test preparation, and the like. She structures programs to meet the needs of individual students."

Anne-Marie knew all about the resource room and didn't want any part of it. "It's still the retard wing," she had blurted out. *There; I finally said it.*

Mrs. DeShields had simply laughed at the remark. "Yep, people call it that."

But Anne-Marie's father had still been stuck on square one. He said, "We are talking about a college-bound young woman in her senior year of high school. This is simply no time to be redefining categories."

Her mother said, "But the structured study hall sounds positive. It might give Anne-Marie the guidance she needs to achieve better study habits and better grades."

"Hey!" Anne-Marie had protested. "We're talking about me here. We're talking about *me*."

Mrs. DeShields had been understanding. "Of course we are," she said. "If it's your decision not to take the test, or not to have any connection with the resource room, then I'm certainly not going to force you. I simply think it might be smart to investigate the possibility."

Anne-Marie had been relieved; she couldn't be forced. Mrs. DeShields folded her hands on her desk and addressed the family as one. "I'm sympathetic here, I really am. I can understand your confusion and frustration as a family. Anne-Marie's sister set the bar of academic achievement awfully high."

"Please," Anne-Marie had said. "Don't bring up Eleanor. She's like this giant shadow I can never get out from under."

"I understand. But just a moment, if I may. Anne-Marie, with an ACT score of twenty and a GPA barely above two point zero, your college choices are going to be limited."

"Pretty soon you're going to be talking about junior colleges," her father had interrupted.

"I already am," said the counselor decisively, but politely.

Anne-Marie was on Mrs. DeShields's side at this juncture. "What did you think, Dad?" she had asked. "I was going to get into a good college just because you say so, or just because my older sister is so special?"

"Don't get smart with me."

Mrs. DeShields had moved in again: "Whatever college it turns out to be, wouldn't it be better to try to increase Anne-Marie's chances for success between now and next June if we can?"

"It's hard to argue with that logic," her mother had said to her father.

"Logic? Is that what we're calling it?"

By now Anne-Marie was too crushed to say anything. She'd slumped in her chair and crossed her arms on her chest. "I'm tired of this whole conversation. I don't want to talk about it anymore."

It was Sara Curtis who interrupted the demeaning memory and brought Anne-Marie back to the present. A straight-A student, Sara was one of the runners who took notes from the office to students in class. Not for the first time, Anne-Marie wondered, *Why would that be a reward? You get straight A's so they let you deliver notes?*

"You're not busy right now, huh?" she said to Sara. "I'd like to talk to you."

"Talk away," said Sara, with a smile that revealed her oversized teeth. "But if they want me to deliver a note, I have to go."

"I know, but can you like come a little closer?" Anne-Marie said, while glancing from side to side at the other students. "I just heard that Brother Jackson is leaving," she said in a voice so quiet it was scarcely more than a whisper.

"It's true," said Sara. "He'll be here till Friday, and then he's moving on. It's a bummer, huh?"

"Moving on where?"

"I'm not exactly sure, but I think he said something about Kentucky or Tennessee, basically where the Lord leads him."

Anne-Marie felt numb, a condition that was familiar, but not in this context. Not in connection with an evangelist. Slowly, she took the note from the pocket of her jeans, the one from Vice Principal Rosario. She showed it to Sara.

"Are you here to see him?" asked Sara.

"Yes. But now that I'm here, I want to see you."

"Because this just means you're supposed to see the vice principal sometime soon. It doesn't have to be today."

Anne-Marie looked at the pimples that peppered Sara's forehead. "I know," she answered. "But I need a pass. I'm supposed to be in biology right now."

"That's not a problem. Just take your note from Rosario to one of the secretaries. They'll write you one."

"I know." This time she looked into Sara's brown eyes. They were as clear and deep as a mountain pool. Sara couldn't be phony; wouldn't even know how. She could stand around a public school flagpole in group prayer and not care at all what anyone else might think or say. *Will my faith ever be strong enough for that?* Anne-Marie found herself speaking in a whisper: "I've never been very nice to you, have I, Sara?"

The answer didn't come quickly. Sara looked down at the note. "You've never been mean to me, Anne-Marie, if that's what you mean."

"But I've never been nice to you."

"A lot of people have never been nice to me. Maybe they're nice to other people. The whole world can't be nice to you. That's just not realistic."

"I know, but at basketball games, I was cheering and you were in the band. We sat close to each other all the time, but I never tried to be your friend."

"It's okay. You're beautiful. You're popular. There's pressure that goes with that."

She means peer pressure, Anne-Marie thought. If you

were truly a Christian though, getting the approval of your peers would be irrelevant. As long as you had the Lord's approval, nothing else would matter. And for that matter, what good was it to be beautiful and popular if you were also superficial and shallow?

"We called you Bucky," said Anne-Marie matter-of-factly.

"I know," said Sara with a smile. She obviously wasn't self-conscious about her teeth. "But it was mostly during sophomore year and just in the cafeteria."

"We did it more often than that. Brooke and Missy and I. We were mean and cruel. And it was so childish. I think we were jealous of you."

Sara Curtis was the only black member of the student council and a candidate for class valedictorian. She said, "It hurt a little bit, but I mostly just shrugged it off. What was it that made you jealous?"

"Maybe your grades. We knew you would be a valedictorian candidate, and we thought a white person should win that. I'm sorry, Sara. I really mean that." Anne-Marie swallowed hard.

"So exactly what is it you're so sorry for?"

"I'm not exactly sure how to put it into words. For being a dork, I guess. Maybe there were times I hurt you even if it was just ignoring you. . . . Okay, that's it . . . I'm sorry for being a dork." She could feel tears forming.

Sara touched her hand. Anne-Marie flinched only briefly at the moment of contact. "You're new to the Fellowship, Anne-Marie. Don't feel like the Lord is going to convict you all the time."

"I don't want to go through the rest of my life finding sin after sin and spending all my time confessing. I'll just be ashamed all the time."

"You won't have to," Sara assured her. "The Lord will convict you from time to time, just like he does all of us. But mostly He will forgive you. If you put your trust there, He will never let you down. I forgive you and I'm sure the Lord forgave you a long time ago."

"Thank you." For several seconds, Anne-Marie looked into Sara's clear brown reassuring eyes. "I hope you win," she said sincerely.

"Thank you. So do I. But it's not a big deal. I'm already accepted at Oberlin, and I've got some scholarship money coming."

"I'm afraid it's going to be junior college for me," said Anne-Marie glumly.

Sara seemed ready with an answer, but then a secretary summoned her, so she had to make a run. Before she left, she invited Anne-Marie to Bible study, the one she held in her house on Monday nights.

At lunch, Anne-Marie sat with Brooke and Missy Timmons, but her mind was a million miles away. Missy had her term paper for biology finished, and a nice glossy cover of Everglades saw grass she'd made on her computer was the wrap.

Anne-Marie told Missy how good the term paper

looked, but wouldn't permit herself to think about it. Couldn't even if she wanted to. Her mind was on Brother Jackson. Why was he leaving, and would he ever come back? If so, when? Would she ever see him again? Would there be another tabernacle meeting where she could? She chewed at the edges of her taco shell halfheartedly all the while; her appetite was still as borderline as her concentration.

She tried to pay attention in world history, her best subject, but her mind wandered to the vice principal's note. If the note meant that she was getting more unsatisfactory progress reports, then copies would be mailed to her parents. They would probably arrive in the mail today or tomorrow. She would be grounded. She always was when her parents got progress reports.

After school, Anne-Marie found herself driving west, across the Fox on the St. Charles Bridge, headed toward the forest preserve. She needed to see Brother Jackson again, even if it wasn't in the tabernacle setting. If she was grounded, she wouldn't be allowed to go, and he was leaving on Friday. When she was born again, he'd stood at the center of it, like he was the midwife of it, somehow. Her tabernacle experience had been like a celestial concert, with Brother Jackson serving as the conductor of its orchestra. She had heard angels singing.

She found the forest preserve again, but not before she'd taken a couple of wrong turns. It seemed much different in the daylight. The shelter was actually part of a larger complex of buildings; there was a long dining hall made of wood siding, with shutters roped back. Anne-Marie could hear some banging pots and pans and some women talking in loud voices from inside.

It seemed unlikely that such a place could even be here. She knew that upscale suburbs and brutal traffic were only a few hundred yards away in any direction. This complex of crude and simple buildings felt like an oasis in the desert. It was buffered by so many oak and maple trees along such dense rolling acreage, its secluded status seemed sacred. This place was *in* the world, but not *of* the world.

Two geese flew over, loud honkers and big ones. They brought sudden, unwelcome thoughts about her term paper. Anne-Marie dismissed the thoughts; she felt nervous, not knowing where to look, and not knowing what she might say to Brother Jackson even if she found him. In fact, she had to remind herself that he might not even be here this time of day.

Near the clump of maple trees behind some of the cabins were pole sheds that looked like maintenance buildings. She headed that way. Behind one of the sheds, she found him working on the mowing deck of a Ford tractor. He was prying with a large screwdriver; some socket wrenches were scattered close at hand. He was wearing a pair of faded blue jeans but no shirt. As soon as he noticed her standing there, he looked up with a smile. "Hello, Sister."

Anne-Marie blushed. "Hello," was all she could think to say.

"Can I help you?"

Now what? "I went to one of your praise meetings a couple of weeks ago."

"Did it bless you?"

"Yes," Anne-Marie replied quickly, "it did."

"Praise God, okay?"

"It was the first time I'd ever been to a tabernacle meeting. I guess I just wanted to introduce myself."

"So now you're introducing yourself. What's your name?"

"Anne-Marie Morgan. My friend Brooke brought me." She wondered how stupid that sounded. Like Brother Jackson would know who her friends were.

"Praise God. I'm sure the Lord will bless her for it. Are you saved, Anne-Marie?"

She lowered her eyes. The conversation seemed like it was accelerating. "I'm not sure," she mumbled. "I think so now." She was quick to add, "I love the way you preach."

He smiled with glorious teeth, white and straight, before he pushed the brown hair out of his eyes. "Thank you, Sister, but we don't preach. What we do is share the Spirit. Preaching sermons is for the standard-brand churches."

His magnetism wasn't limited to the way he spoke in front of a group. He was so easy to talk to. "I think I know what you mean. My parents wouldn't approve of praise meetings."

Brother Jackson didn't lose his smile. "No surprise in that, Anne-Marie. What we do is much too bold for people who like their church life respectable and lukewarm. But tell me, what do *you* approve of?"

"I'd like to receive the gifts of the Spirit," she answered. "My friend Sara Curtis speaks in tongues."

"And do you want the gift of tongues?"

"Just some gift of the Spirit," she answered quickly. "It wouldn't have to be tongues, Brother Jackson. Up until a few weeks ago, I didn't know anything at all about gifts of the Spirit." Now the conversation was in thoroughly uncharted territory, but something about him gave her the courage to voice these untested notions.

"The gifts come when we don't seek them. That's why they are gifts—they come from God's grace." He stopped speaking long enough to drink water from a quart jar. Sweat ran in rivulets down the surface of his lean torso.

Anne-Marie watched him with fascination. He was a blend of sublime spirit and earthy, physical strength. It was the unlikely combination that captivated her. *How old is he?* she wondered. *Maybe thirty-something,* she guessed.

When he drank with his head turned, she tried to pull her long hair back. Doing so, though, and glancing down to watch her blouse sliding up to expose a generous amount of her midriff, she became self-conscious about the silver hoop piercing the fold of her navel. *Would he think it was pagan or idolatrous? Would he think it childish?* Quickly, she pushed her top back down. She asked him why he was doing this mechanic's work.

"Our crusade is only here for a few weeks," he answered. "It can't hurt me to do a little nuts and bolts for the good of the facility."

"I thought all of this belonged to the forest preserve."

"You're right, but the campground association has a lease agreement. Taking care of the grounds is part of the agreement, I believe."

"But what does it have to do with the crusade?"

"It has everything to do with the crusade. The Lord blesses all our efforts when they are sincere."

Anne-Marie stared at his well-formed right arm, the one holding the water jar. The sweat seemed to highlight the definition of his muscles. Brother Jackson continued by saying, "Working in the Lord's vineyards might just as well take us into every nook and cranny where there is honorable labor. Even if it be slopping hogs or chopping weeds. Many of the disciples were simple fishermen, or have I forgotten my Bible?" Now he was laughing.

Anne-Marie knew she couldn't keep up. Not with his knowledge, nor even with her own feelings. Resting in the small patch of black chest hair, just above his sternum, was a small silver cross attached to a slender rawhide strand. She cleared her throat before she said, "The church my parents go to is suits and ties only."

"The church your parents go to?"

"Well, I used to go there, too. They'd be a lot happier if I still did."

"The Bible says the Lord loves a glad heart. He who serves with a glad heart. It doesn't say anything much about suits and ties or fingernail polish."

"That's what I believe," she was quick to agree. "People are too hung up on what they can see on the surface."

Brother Jackson was using a gray shop rag to clean the grease from around his fingernails. "Sister," he said, "how 'bout if I show you around?"

"Sure, why not."

There wasn't much to show. There was an old greenhouse with too many broken windows and a large shop which was home to lawn tractors and air compressors. On the back side of the shop was his room.

"This is where you stay?" she asked him.

"This is home, Sister. For the past few weeks, this is where I've been hanging my hat."

Anne-Marie doubted if he ever wore a hat, except maybe a baseball cap. "For how many weeks?"

"I've been here four," Brother Jackson answered. "Friday is my last day."

"Won't it make you sad to leave?"

"The beauty of serving the Lord is that He makes the schedule and all we have to do is follow." He was smiling.

"Where are you going from here?"

"I'm off to a crusade in Indiana for a while. I'll be taking a tour in the Hoosier state."

Anne-Marie couldn't imagine how much faith it would

take to move around from state to state with no guarantees. She was young in the Fellowship, though; she felt confident the Lord wouldn't convict her when she had doubts.

The room was small, and relatively dark, for there was only one window, which was partially obscured by a box fan resting on the sill. The simple rollaway bed was neatly made. A wooden chair was in the corner next to a table with a reading lamp. On the table was a well-worn Bible. A big poster on the wall with the words *El Shaddai* showed a picture of a mountain peak piercing the clouds.

Just standing there in his room without talking made her tense. "What does El Shaddai mean?" she asked him.

"It means the Good Lord Himself," was the answer.

They were speaking in the lowest of voices. When she reached to pull down on the hem of her blouse, she felt her arm brush against his skin. She was practically dazed at the turbulence of her emotions at this moment. She felt electrified, body and soul.

She needed to say something. "I like your cross," she told him, with her eyes lowered.

"This cross?" Brother Jackson asked. He took it off. "It's nothing special, I've had it for years."

"But it looks so delicate and so . . . so simple."

"The world is full of nice crosses to wear." Then he chuckled. "You know what, Sister? I almost said nice crosses to *bear*." He had his pocket knife out by this time and was cutting through the rawhide strip with a sawing motion.

"What are you doing?" Anne-Marie asked.

"If you like the cross, then you should have it."

"Oh, I couldn't do that."

"And why not?" He turned to face her, again with the smile.

"But how could I just take your cross?"

"By receiving it as a gift. By trusting me when I tell you it isn't something I cherish." The cross was in the palm of his hand. It was plain and silver, approximately three quarters of an inch long and half as wide.

When Anne-Marie looked up from the cross, she met his eyes. It wasn't the argument about accepting the gift that perplexed her, but something else. It was the current flowing through her veins. At this moment, the one and only thing clear in her head was that she craved his approval. "Just trust you?" she asked.

"Trust what I tell you," he repeated. "How will you be open to receive the gifts of the Spirit if you have such a hard time accepting a trinket?"

"Where would I wear it?" She didn't feel like she was controlling the words coming out of her own mouth.

"Why not let me put it on you?" Saying this, Brother Jackson began to lift the hem of her top. Anne-Marie shivered, but didn't recoil. Quickly and efficiently, he worked the small ring in the top of the cross through the tight aperture of her belly button loop. His fingers traveled against her skin. There was no pain; he was careful not to pull her flesh.

It felt to Anne-Marie like some divinely mystical moment, his fixing the cross to part of her own body, as it were. Like a consecration or an ordination.

When he took her, it was on the simple bed. Before he made his swift but gentle entry, Brother Jackson applied oil to himself, which he took from a bottle on the window ledge. *Does he think this is my first time? But what oil would this be, and why is it so handy?*

But her hypnotic condition seemed to activate a series of dreamlike, open-ended thoughts. Some of them blended with scattered scripture . . . *Thou anointest my head with oil. . . .*

Her submission in the shape of open, lifted thighs formed a valley to receive the secret shaft like an arrow to the soul. . . . *Yea, though I walk through the valley . . .* The silver cross, she couldn't help noticing each time he lifted himself, rested on her abdomen just above her tan line like an imprimatur.

May 11

Her watch said 7:40 A.M. when Anne-Marie picked a parking space in the school lot. Even though it was only twenty minutes before first-hour classes, empty spaces were abundant. She'd never found a place so close before. It was a warm, mild morning, which she took as an invitation from God.

Today she would find the courage to join the prayer group around the flagpole.

To make herself inconspicuous, she walked a circuitous route between parked cars so she could emerge close to the gathering. She was very anxious; but Coleen moved immediately to make room for her in the circle, reaching out her hand. "Praise God, Anne-Marie, come and join us."

"Thank you," Anne-Marie replied. "I didn't know if I could find the courage."

"It won't take as much courage as you might think," said a junior named Hiram. "The fellowship is strong, as strong as a fortress," he added.

She held hands with Coleen and Hiram, whose last name she didn't know. Hiram was pimply, with a strong body odor that added to the queasiness in her stomach. The queasy stomach, a regular visitor these days, felt like it had a life of its own. This nervous knot was not connected to any conflict with her parents, or any academic screwups.

It was with stinging guilt that Anne-Marie remembered the time she and two other cheerleaders had hidden Hiram's French horn and put a bottle of Clearasil in its case. She wanted to tell him how sorry she was, but she was so new to this flagpole fellowship, she wasn't ready to speak yet.

But holding hands—even Hiram's—to form the circle was surprisingly nonthreatening, in spite of the public exposure that gave the drive-by students opportunities to spew out their taunts and catcalls:

Hey children! Better look up in the sky!
Jesus may be in a landing pattern!

Oh Jesus, I've got a chemistry test today.
Can you fly down and take it for me? Please?

The bond in the circle was strong enough that Anne-Marie could largely ignore the contempt. The queasiness dissipated, replaced by a firm sense of security. In the Lord there was safety. *I am strong enough to be here and strong enough to do this.*

Chris Weems stood on the other side. He was tall, but

thin and pale. His eyes were closed, his face lifted up to bathe in the warm, early morning sun. He looked at peace, but Anne-Marie knew from her conversations with Brooke that he had an inner conflict about being gay. *Maybe he's praying about that right now,* she thought.

Sara was already praying out loud, "Dear Jesus, we find our strength in you. The contemptuous behavior of the contemptible can't shake the refuge we find in You. We pray You to lift us higher than their need to persecute."

Contemptuous behavior of the contemptible. She's so good with words, Anne-Marie thought, *even in front of a group.*

Then a girl named Hanna said, "We pray for them too, though. We ask you to enter their hearts so they too will enter Your state of grace. We ask you to lead them into the Fellowship of True Believers."

"Amen," said several of the others. Anne-Marie said it too. "Amen." She felt it. The taunters were poor souls needing rescue; she found herself pitying them rather than resenting them. A sudden surge of generosity of spirit flooded her, sweeping away the last small scraps of nerves. It felt like purification.

Chris Weems said softly, "I need forgiveness for a sin. Can you please help me pray for forgiveness?"

"What's your sin?" someone asked.

"My younger brother takes clothes out of my closet. He wears them without my permission. I've told him lots of times to stop, but he keeps taking what he wants and wearing it. It makes me angry."

"The Lord won't convict you for being mad," Hanna said. "All you have to do is forgive your brother and then ask the Lord to forgive you."

"Yesterday, though," said Chris—his eyes were closed again—"I drove to school and left him behind on purpose. He doesn't have his license yet. He had to walk to school. I did it to pay him back."

"Have you told him you're sorry?" someone asked.

"Yes. Twice."

"Have you prayed with him?"

"No. He's not a believer. He's not interested in the Fellowship."

"Then ask for God's forgiveness," said Sara.

"That's what I'm doing right now," Chris replied quickly. "I'm asking the group to pray with me."

"Praise God for it," said Coleen. "Praise Him for your submission."

"Thank you."

"We all pray for your forgiveness," said Sara. "The Word assures us that when we make a sincere confession, the sin is forgiven."

"Amen," said several in the circle. "Praise God," said Anne-Marie quietly. She looked at Chris; his eyes were open again. But he had tears; she saw them on his cheeks even though he was thirty feet away.

The wind whipped the flag's draw-cord so that it made a steady slap-slap-slapping against the silver pole. But Anne-

Marie was centered; she scarcely noticed the noise. Not even the honking of the Canada goose that glided overhead could distract her.

She was ready to make a public confession of how she'd been a part of teasing and taunting Hiram in the past. She wanted to apologize and ask for his forgiveness. But Hiram had begun to mutter in syllables she couldn't understand. His voice crescendoed up and then back down; it was something like singing or chanting, but not in words.

He's speaking in tongues, Anne-Marie thought. *He is blessed with gifts of the Spirit.* It was the first time she'd heard anyone speak in tongues and it seemed absolutely cosmic, as if Hiram had found a sublime plane of light which no human cruelty could touch or darken. Anne-Marie shivered while she gripped his hand tighter.

You didn't have to speak out loud while praying around the flagpole. In fact, most people didn't. But Anne-Marie felt so secure in her inner glow of grace, she found herself repeating a Bible verse she had reflected on the night before. "'Whither though goest, I will go,'" she said slowly.

"Praise God."

"Thank you, Sister."

The immediate approval emboldened her. She went on to finish the passage, which she had now committed to memory: "'Thy people shall be my people, and thy God shall be my God.'" Then she was quiet. Her eyes were tightly shut. The others were confessing sins or conflicts, but she was merely quoting passages of Scripture. Yet she felt unequivocal acceptance anyway; the Fellowship had lots of doors and thresholds. Rejection was alien to all the circle stood for.

She felt a tiny bit queasy again as Coleen squeezed her hand. "The Lord will bless you for this," her friend told her.

"I think He already has," Anne-Marie replied.

Third hour, she got a summons to the counseling office from Mrs. DeShields. Her heart dropped to her stomach, which once again had a dull, minor ache. The residual effects of prayer around the flagpole, however, had given her a sense of pride and promise. Anne-Marie didn't even bother to wait for the resource room to empty out. Instead, she left class with the other students, oblivious to who might or might not see her leaving the LD room.

But the knot began forming in her stomach again, despite the promise and approval of the morning's prayer circle. Chris Weems was there before Anne-Marie arrived, sitting at one of the round tables in the waiting room. "What're you doing here?" she asked him. "I thought you never got in trouble."

He smiled, but not with any real mirth. Though he smiled with his mouth, his deep, doe-brown eyes didn't change. Even though she didn't know him very well, suddenly, Anne-Marie remembered his liquid brown eyes vividly, as if she had actually made a past practice of scanning them.

"You were at the prayer circle this morning," said Chris.

"Yeah, I was."

"First time?"

"Yep, first time."

"How'd you like it?" he asked.

"It was fine. I was touched and moved. It wasn't nearly as scary as I thought it might be."

Chris leaned back in his chair, his eyes as deep as pools, but neutral. Anne-Marie thought how good he must be at masking his true feelings, but wondered if it came naturally. Maybe it came with lots of practice. From her talks with Brooke she knew the real pain in his heart was about being gay. "So what clothes did your brother want to borrow?" she asked him.

"It's not what he *wanted* to borrow, it's what he *did* borrow. Actually, *stealing* might be a better word than borrowing, because if you borrow something it means you've asked for permission."

"What clothes?"

"Sweaters mostly."

"But you're so tall, Chris. How would they fit your smaller brother?"

"They don't fit. He just likes them, and the looser the better."

"I never had the problem," said Anne-Marie. "My sister, Eleanor, was six years older. I couldn't have worn her clothes even if I'd wanted to. But when she moved away from home for college and grad school, she left a lot of her finest behind. It practically doubled my wardrobe." Anne-Marie wasn't thinking about clothes, though. She was thinking about Chris.

He might have felt a little guilty about leaving his younger brother at home without a ride to school, but she knew that wasn't his core suffering. Anne-Marie had the sudden urge to ask him about it, but she didn't know him well enough. *That doesn't make sense,* she thought; *when we're connected in the Fellowship, we're bonded more tightly than any mere friendship, even a very close one.*

"We get stronger when we're joined together with the Fellowship of believers," he said.

"Huh?"

"You said joining the circle around the flagpole wasn't nearly as scary as you thought it might be. I'm just telling you why I think that is. There's strength in numbers."

"Oh, right. You're right. It's the togetherness." She stopped talking long enough to tighten her black scrunchie. "I've been reading my Bible a lot, too," she told him. "When we were holding hands, I repeated the verse, 'If God be for us, who can be against us?' It's from Romans."

"It's the perfect passage," said Chris, nodding his head swiftly. "Romans eight, verse thirty-one."

"You know that by heart?" She was amazed.

"It's a familiar passage," he replied. "I repeat it often myself." He leaned forward again and propped his elbows on the table.

"You never told me why you're here," Anne-Marie reminded him. "Are you in some kind of trouble?"

He smiled again. "No, no trouble. I've just been working with Mrs. Kaplan on a scholarship application to Northwestern."

"With your high grades, why would you have any trouble getting in?"

"How do you know about my grades?"

"You're in the National Honor Society," Anne-Marie answered immediately.

"I'm not worried about being accepted, I have been already. But I need scholarship money, or my family can't afford to send me there."

His academic problems couldn't possibly be any more different than mine. He's choosing from prestigious colleges and I'm probably not even going to graduate.

Then he asked her, "Why are you here?"

It was so embarrassing. But she felt confident in his company. "I've got to talk to Mrs. DeShields. I think she's written up a performance contract for me and my parents to sign. Chris, I might not graduate on time."

"Oh, Anne-Marie, I'm so sorry. Are you sure about this?"

"Pretty sure. I don't know what else it could be."

"Can I help you at all?" He reached over and put his right hand on top of her left one. His hand was soft and moist.

"I wouldn't know how," she replied.

"Can I help you with any work sheets or tests or reports?" he asked.

He was obviously kind and sincere, but Anne-Marie could feel her eyes tearing up. "I may have to go to summer school," was all she could say.

"I'll pray for you," said Chris.

"Thank you. People were praying for me and with me this morning," she observed. "I felt so much *acceptance* and so . . . so cleansed. Why would I have to get a performance contract on the very same day?"

"The Lord won't love you any less," said Chris. "He doesn't love us based on our grade point averages."

"I know," she said. "But it doesn't seem to help right now, not if I'm about to be put on contract."

Chris squeezed her hand. "Try to remember the Lord loves you just as much as a valedictorian."

"Thank you. I will try to remember."

In Mrs. DeShields's office, Anne-Marie got a good long look at the performance contract. With escalating anxiety, she took the single sheet from its manila mailer, which was already addressed to her parents. She noticed there wasn't any postage on it, though. With only a few minor surprises, the contract was what she had expected. Mrs. DeShields was the counselor she trusted most, but the formal language of the document—and the fact it was also to be signed by Vice Principal Rosario—still left her numb.

She forced herself to read through its terms. Mrs. DeShields was thoughtful enough to turn her back and work; Anne-Marie was grateful she could read without the pressure of being "under surveillance." The document said that in order to graduate, she would need to complete English and biology in the summer school program, with no grade lower than a B.

She would be expected to attend each and every class session without exception. She would be expected to turn in all homework assignments on time, including essays, folder work, and work sheets. If necessary, there was a provision for make-up tests, if she failed one or got a low grade.

At the bottom was a paragraph declaring that she had read the terms of the contract, understood each of them, and also understood that failure to live up to any part of the document would mean failure to graduate. Mrs. DeShields had already signed the contract, since she was the one who had drawn it up. There were four other lines for signatures, one for the vice principal, one for herself, and one for each of her parents.

She read through the document a second time, but none of the language changed. It felt so degrading. Of all the academic rebukes she'd ever received, this was the most humiliating, even more so than the LD resource room. At school, if you were put on a contract, you were a dork. No, worse than a dork; you were a jerk. Contracts were for special ed people, behavior disordered, or at-risk students. People who were so screwed up they had to be in the alternative school.

Or even worse, contracts were often for students with criminal records who were in school while on probation.

Mrs. DeShields turned to face her. "Well, what do you think, Anne-Marie? Do you think this is a contract we can work with?"

"I feel humiliated," she answered immediately.

"I can understand that, but try to think of it as an opportunity as well."

"How can I? I feel like a criminal."

"Try to think of the contract as a focus factor. You know exactly what the demands are, timetable, and so forth. You can even go through graduation ceremonies with the rest of your class."

"I wouldn't want to. It would seem too phony."

Mrs. DeShields paused long enough to bend a paper clip out of shape. "Is it the same kind of humiliation you felt last fall when we tested you for ADD?"

"Yes, only worse. This seems so final."

"Final is what we want. Final is what we'll get. The contract will help you in that respect."

Anne-Marie felt tears forming again, but she refused to shed any. She'd been bathed in the light of the Lord earlier in the morning, but the contract made her feel unworthy. Was God convicting her for pride? Would He show you a beautiful sunrise only to hide it behind a dense cloud cover? She remembered Chris's words of support: The Lord loves you just as much as a valedictorian

Mrs. DeShields went on, "You were embarrassed about the resource room experiment, but did it help you?"

Anne-Marie sighed before she answered. "Yes. It did."

"You got B's in American history and Effective Living. What do you think your grades in those courses would've been without the resource room?"

"I know, I know. They'd have been lower. Everybody gets high grades in Effective Living, though. That's a B we can't really count."

"Oh yes, we can count it," answered the counselor swiftly. "Many students get low grades in Effective Living, because they don't take it seriously or put forth any effort."

Anne-Marie was perusing the contract again. She wanted to change the subject. "Mrs. DeShields, these classes all meet in the evening or late in the afternoon. Why is that?"

"Many students who take summer school classes have full-time jobs. Some of them are even adults working on getting their GED."

Anne-Marie didn't know what a GED was, and she didn't really care to find out. But all of a sudden the humiliation was acute again. She implored the counselor, "Mrs. DeShields, please; I've got ten days left, isn't there some way I could get this work done on time?"

"Anne-Marie, let me turn the question straight back at you. For instance, where do you stand on your biology term paper?"

The Canada geese again. *God, I wish I'd never even heard of them.* "I'm still stumped," was all she could say.

"Don't you think you can make better progress on it in

summer school? You'll have lots more time to work on it, and you'll only have one other course to worry about. And by the way, Mrs. Walls is willing to give you an incomplete rather than a failing grade."

It was a hollow victory. Mrs. DeShields might be making sense, but the disgrace Anne-Marie felt overwhelmed her. Tears began forming again, but she blinked them back. "Mrs. DeShields, do you think I'm a retard?"

"Of course not. And I know we've used that word for teasing, but we should stop it. *Retard* is a slur word; it's demeaning. I think you have a mild learning disorder based on your ADD, but it's certainly not going to cripple you."

"Does this have to be mailed to my parents?"

"Now Anne-Marie."

"I was just hoping . . ."

"Unfortunately, yes it does." Mrs. DeShields was legalistic but somehow supportive at the same time. "You know it's school policy that performance contracts be signed by a parent or guardian."

"When will you mail it?"

"It won't be for a little while yet. We are processing others right now and we're on overload with state-mandated standardized testing. It could be a couple of weeks."

"It could be after finals then?"

"It's possible."

She left the counseling center about twenty minutes before the fourth-hour passing bell would sound. She could spend the time in the library before she headed for lunch. Her stomach was roiling; she felt she'd crossed the threshold to join the Body of Christ earlier, then the contract, which was absolutely mortifying. When she got to the library door again, she whispered last night's passage: "'If God be for us, who can be against us?'"

She could get through this because she wasn't alone. The light of God's Kingdom would illuminate the darkness and the shadows. It would be in His time, though, not hers.

June 2

She was sick again, for the second day in a row.

By 6:30 A.M. she had thrown up in the toilet a third time. The only breakfast she'd eaten, the glazed donut, was floating in the bowl along with the gross scent of barf. Her mouth was disgusting with the rancid aftertaste. The nausea made her miserable, but at least there was privacy, because she had the upstairs bathroom all to herself.

She stood up to examine her waxen face in the medicine cabinet mirror. For the third time this morning, she brushed her teeth, and rinsed with Scope. Hidden behind the mouthwash bottle was an EPT home pregnancy test, which she hadn't found the nerve to try yet. She was still woozy, and her head ached, but at least the nausea was past.

Anne-Marie knew she was pregnant. She had no doubts at all. For the past three weeks, each time she got up in the morning, she was woozy and nauseous. Sometimes for an hour or two, sometimes longer. It would be ironic to become pregnant by her one intimate encounter with Brother Jackson, when she'd had unprotected sex with Richard Bone more times than she would want to admit. But that was all too long ago; she'd had several normal period cycles since she'd let herself be seduced by him. As soon as she washed her face, she went downstairs. Her mother was in the master bedroom, applying makeup.

Looking out through the window, Anne-Marie could see the hired hands making preparations for her sister Eleanor's royal reception. It would be a big surprise to Eleanor, but not to Anne-Marie; she was long accustomed to her big sister's position in the limelight.

Eleanor would be surprised and embarrassed by the crowded party on the lawn, the photographers from the *West Suburban Times*, and the choice buffet provided by Van Meter Catering. There was even a string quartet unloading instruments from their van.

By the time the limo which brought Eleanor from O'Hare Airport glided to its stop in front of their home, Anne-Marie was quarreling with her mother. The quarrel was not intense, because the shouting matches were a thing of the past, now that Anne-Marie had found the Lord. Before, she had always been in the prison of her own selfish willfulness.

Watching the limo from the window, and the flock of people who greeted it, Anne-Marie was reminded of the parable of the Prodigal Son. But even the Prodigal Son wouldn't get a reception like this. *My father wouldn't think the*

Prodigal Son deserved anything other than a good whipping and maybe thirty hours of community service.

She knew the time was short. "If I miss this class Monday," she told her mother, "I can make it up the next day. Lots of people do that."

"Maybe that's a part of *their* contract, then," her mother replied.

"It's got nothing to do with a contract," Anne-Marie explained. "It's just a procedure for making up missed classes. Not everybody in summer school is on a contract, Mother."

"But you are, though, remember?"

"Not officially, though. There's no contract in writing yet."

"Don't sound like an attorney, okay?"

"I live with an attorney, remember? I'm just saying we don't have anything official yet from the school."

"But we'll be receiving it soon."

"I mean, Monday is just an orientation meeting. I've had my orientation face-to-face with Mrs. DeShields. Remember?"

"How could I forget? I was there."

"That's my point," Anne-Marie tried to explain. "You know that I'm acquainted with all the details."

"All the details we know about," replied her mother. "There may be more. There may be a syllabus, or other printed material."

"Mother, this might be different if I was just looking for

a place to hang out or goof off. All I'm asking for is permission to fellowship with the Lord."

Her mother was looking into the dressing table mirror while trying to adjust a stubborn earring. "Don't play the holy card, Anne-Marie. I doubt if that will be a strategy that works."

"I'm not playing cards, I'm just telling you the truth."

"There will be lots of other chances for Bible study groups, I'm sure."

"But not with Sara's group. It only meets on Monday nights."

"Then maybe somebody else's study group, hmm? Or maybe just plain old church on Sunday morning. I feel confident that the Lord makes His presence known in settings other than Sara Curtis's family room."

Why should I expect my mother to understand? But how could she, when all she knew of religion was the watered-down and the lukewarm? What could she know of the bold, the born-again, or the Spirit-filled life? She couldn't be expected to understand something so transforming, so passionate. It would have been even less likely for her mother to understand the complex relationship she had with Brother Jackson or the tiny snail of life turning in her womb. *Must* be turning. How else could she explain the morning sickness?

Her mother had the earring in place and was ready to join the reception. "I can't talk about this now, Anne-Marie. We'll have to table it until later. We'll discuss it with your father."

That was the death sentence for sure, since her father was even more rigid than her mother. She needed to set her own needs aside, though, because this was Eleanor's day, not hers.

Most of the reception was on the front lawn, although the driveway was available as well because her father had gotten permission to move his restored Jaguar and the old Chevy into a neighbor's driveway. The tent on the lawn turned out to be unnecessary; the day was glorious with warm sun and very little breeze. Some people sat beneath it, however, to get out of the bright light.

Eleanor gave Anne-Marie a quick hug of greeting, but then was swallowed up by well-wishers and media. A number of the city's leading citizens were there, as well as a Republican state representative named DiGregorio, to whom her father made yearly campaign contributions.

By the time the strings commenced with selections from Vivaldi and Mozart, Anne-Marie was helping herself to mushrooms and scooping them in a mellow, cheesy dip which seemed to go down easy.

When her stomach began feeling touchy again, she finished with the mushroom dipping, tied off a couple of full garbage bags, then went inside the house. She watched the proceedings from the living room window. She was happy for her sister's stunning success and recognition, as she knew the Lord would want her to be, but she herself was grounded. The whole scene reminded her of her own history of paltry achievement in comparison to her older sister's.

Her father had now gathered all those assembled into a

sort of semicircle, while someone Anne-Marie didn't know was extolling the praises of Eleanor's winning the Oneppo Medal, a symbol of the highest academic esteem in the entire universe.

Other people were scheduled to add a few remarks, Dad included, and the media would interview Eleanor, but Anne-Marie went to get the mail. There were two letters for her, one from a Junior college and another from the high school. She took them upstairs to her room. Her television was on, playing a rerun of a cable religious program in which Billy Graham Junior was interviewing a born-again woman who was a former drug addict. Anne-Marie's television was nowadays tuned to Channel 14 almost exclusively. She turned it off.

With escalating anxiety, she tore open the letter from the high school. It was what she expected—the contract for summer school. It had Vice Principal Rosario's signature now as well.

It wasn't until the early part of the evening that Anne-Marie got to spend some private time with Eleanor on the sunporch. The caterers were still cleaning up, but nearly finished. "Can I see your medal?" asked Anne-Marie.

"Sure." Eleanor handed over the medal, resting on its cushion of velvet in its open black box. It was large, maybe two inches from top to bottom, a clear crystal in the shape of a teardrop. In the center was a three-sided obelisk, which looked like granite or marble, suspended magically to form an elongated, glittering pyramid in three dimensions. When

Anne-Marie held it up to the window, in the evening light, its center bent the light like a colorful prism. She hoped it wasn't a pagan thing, because it was truly breathtaking.

"Do you have a chain for it?" Anne-Marie asked her.

"Not that I know of," was Eleanor's reply.

"Then how will you wear it?"

"I don't think it's a medal for wearing, Baby. Where would you wear it? The Oneppo Medal is only for show, I'm afraid."

"It should be for show because it's so beautiful," Anne-Marie replied. Jealousy reared its ugly head again. She put the medal back inside the box.

"It's only an academic award and not worth all this commotion," said Eleanor. She meant the press conference, of course, and the reception. Eleanor had changed into a pair of faded blue jeans and a Harvard sweatshirt. She stretched and yawned before adding, "Lots of people win academic awards, but they don't have parents with resources or access to the press."

It was a typical Eleanor remark. So utterly self-confident she felt no need to show off anything for anybody. The medal might just as well have been a plastic trinket from the bottom of a Cracker Jack box. What the medal meant was that Eleanor was top of her class in the MBA program at the University of Chicago, which won her a full fellowship at Harvard Law School. What it meant to Anne-Marie was the most recent symbol of Eleanor's spectacularly successful life.

As she handed back the box, Anne-Marie tried to guard against the envy. The envy was a habit but it didn't need to be, not anymore. The Bible warned not to covet; it didn't say anything specific about coveting your sister's life, but Anne-Marie felt certain that was meant to be part of the meaning. Then, without even realizing it, she had started to cry.

"Baby, you're crying. What's wrong?"

She wasn't sobbing, but there were tears sliding down her cheeks. She tried wiping them with the back of her hand before she said, "Nothing. Besides, this is your day."

"I've had more of *my day* than I can endure," said Eleanor with contempt. She made a sour face like she'd just taken a bite out of a lemon. "Tell me what's wrong."

"I'm pregnant," said Anne-Marie quickly, before her constricted throat could choke her.

"Oh no. Oh dear." Eleanor put her arm around Anne-Marie's shoulder. "Come here." Anne-Marie let her head drop to Eleanor's shoulder, but her tears began to flow again immediately.

"Who's the father?"

Anne-Marie could only shake her head. She didn't want to try to explain the Brother Jackson circumstance, and besides, she was ashamed of shifting the focus from Eleanor to herself. It took nearly three minutes of tear-wiping and nose-blowing before she recovered enough composure to start answering Eleanor's questions.

"Are you sure?" Eleanor wanted to know.

"I'm sure," she said, with her head still nuzzled into Eleanor's sweatshirt.

"How are you sure?"

"I took one of those home pregnancy tests. I got it at the drugstore." *The Lord hates a liar, so why do I do it?*

"Not good enough, Baby. Not reliable enough."

"But it says so, right on the package."

"Not good enough. You need to go to a clinic for a real examination."

"Huh?"

"I said, home pregnancy tests won't cut it. You need to visit a clinic."

"I know I probably should."

"And not just to confirm that you're pregnant, either. You need to get a complete examination if you are."

"I know I should," Anne-Marie said again.

"What do you plan to do about it?" Eleanor asked her.

Anne-Marie looked up to meet her sister's gray-green eyes. Nobody could listen like Eleanor, nobody ever could. "I don't know. I just get confused."

"We need to visit a place like Planned Parenthood or the Women's Support Network. You need to know all your options and you need to understand all the health issues."

Anne-Marie nodded but didn't answer. She buried her face again in the fresh lilac smell of her big sister's arm. She knew Eleanor's advice would be perfect.

"A big part of the confusion comes from not having enough information," Eleanor was explaining. "The more knowledge you have, the less scary the dilemma." She was stroking Anne-Marie's hair and pulling the wet strands out of her eyes.

Anne-Marie had a fleeting thought of Brother Jackson, long enough to wish she could introduce him to Eleanor, but knowing all the same that she wouldn't understand or appreciate him. It felt so sad when important parts of your life didn't fit together.

"I'll help you," Eleanor promised. "Tomorrow, we'll do some networking until we can get the kind of help we need. Try not to worry too much; there are choices and options."

Eleanor's advice couldn't have been more appropriate or sincere, but Anne-Marie understood the relief it provided was dead-end. The perfection was the problem. She was the unworthy sinner, pregnant and confused, while her big sister was perfect.

June 4

On Monday morning Anne-Marie found herself with an acute case of nerves before Eleanor even chose a space in the hot parking lot. The Planned Parenthood clinic was a long, single-story building of white brick, set at the end of a strip mall with a Papa John's Pizza and a huge Walgreen's. There were a few people on the corner, walking while holding large signs. One of the signs read:

ABORTION IS MURDER!

Another one read:

A CHILD IS NOT A CHOICE!

"Eleanor, there's no way I could go in here if they do abortions. I could never have an abortion."

"We're not here to get an abortion," Eleanor replied. "We're only here to get you some counseling."

"Because the Lord would never condone an abortion. It's a sin, it's like a murder."

"If you don't want to have an abortion, no one is going to make you. Did you hear what I just said? We're only here to get some counseling. Now don't be silly; get out of the car."

The waiting room was air-conditioned and comfortable. The two sisters sat in padded chairs while waiting for a nurse named Mrs. Howard. There was a coffee table with stacks of literature and pamphlets dealing with pregnancy, prenatal care, assurances of confidentiality, and parenting.

Together, they browsed through a red leaflet called, *Am I Parent Material?* There were several pages of questions with cartoonish drawings as illustrations of dilemmas and choices. Some of the questions were obvious ones, such as, "Could I handle a child and a job at the same time? Would I have time and energy enough for both?"

The more disturbing questions in the pamphlet were under a heading called, *Have my partner and I really talked about becoming parents?* The first question in this section was *Does my partner want to have a child? Have we talked about our reasons?*

"Please put this away," said Anne-Marie abruptly. "I don't want to look at it anymore." She hadn't told Brother Jackson she was pregnant, and it was something she didn't want to think about. She hadn't even seen him since that afternoon they were intimate. He was far away in Crawfordsville, Indiana. She felt her nerves on the rise again; only her sister's presence kept her from heading straight for the parking lot.

Their wait was a short one. Mrs. Howard invited them into her office five minutes later. She was a young black woman with an RN badge pinned to her blouse, so young she looked like she couldn't be much older than Eleanor. She folded her hands on her desktop before she asked, "So. Why are we here? What can we do to help?"

Anne-Marie glanced nervously in Eleanor's direction, but her big sister looked away. *She's putting the ball in my court,* Anne-Marie was quick to realize. She cleared her throat before she said, "I'm pregnant. I'm pregnant, but I could never have an abortion."

Mrs. Howard smiled. "Fair enough. Nobody would try to convince you to have one if your mind is made up."

"My mind is made up."

"Fine. That's that, then."

"And I have to know that everything we talk about is completely confidential. My parents don't know and if anybody ends up telling them, it has to be me."

"I can assure you that anything you say will be held in absolute confidence. Nothing we do or say here will be shared with anyone else, okay?"

"And that's for sure?"

"That's for sure. Here's a statement of our confidentiality policy." The nurse passed a paper across the desk in Anne-Marie's direction. "The same confidentiality rules that apply to others will apply to you. May I ask how old you are, Anne-Marie?"

"Seventeen. I won't turn eighteen until the end of August."

"That makes you seventeen and three quarters, then. But still a minor. Let me ask you, first of all, why you think you're pregnant."

"I took one of those home pregnancy tests, the kind you get at the drugstore." *The same lie again? Why?* Maybe because it didn't sound as stupid as saying, *I just know I am; I can just tell.*

"Do you understand that those are occasionally not accurate? When was your last period?"

"The first of April."

"One thing we do ask each client to do is take a pregnancy test here, to be sure we know what we're talking about. It's a simple urinalysis, and we can get the results in just a few minutes. Do you feel up to that?"

Anne-Marie glanced in Eleanor's direction again, but her big sister was looking over the confidentiality statement. Then Anne-Marie looked back at Nurse Howard. "Would this be in confidence, too?"

"Of course. Everything we do here will be in strict confidence."

"Go ahead," Eleanor joked. "You've peed in a bottle before."

"Okay, okay." Anne-Marie giggled, in spite of herself. She had peed in a bottle before, a time or two for cheerleader drug testing, in addition to other ordinary doctor visits.

This part was easy, because Anne-Marie felt like she was about to wet her pants anyway. When the specimen bottle was full, she washed her hands thoroughly before she gave it to Mrs. Howard. The nurse handed it to a lab technician, then took Anne-Marie back to her office.

"While we're waiting for the test results, I'd like to ask you a few lifestyle questions," she said to Anne-Marie.

"Okay."

"If it turns out you are pregnant, one of the first things you need to do is pay attention to your health habits. Do you smoke?"

"No," she answered quickly. But she could feel Eleanor's eyes boring in from her left side, so she added, "Not anymore. I used to smoke with this boyfriend I had."

"Good. No smoking. Any drugs?"

"No." She could have added the same proviso with respect to the Richard part of her life, but she decided to keep the answers simple. Besides, all she ever did with him was smoke some cigarettes with a little rock powder inside the tobacco.

"You will want to watch your diet. One of the simplest good habits is to eat plenty of fruits and vegetables, especially leafy ones like lettuce and cabbage."

"I like salads," said Anne-Marie.

"Good. They provide you with plenty of folic acid, which is important for women who are pregnant."

Anne-Marie tried to remember if anyone had ever called her a woman before. The nurse asked her, "Are you taking any medication?"

"No. Sometimes I take aspirin when I get headaches. Or Alka-Seltzer when my stomach is upset."

Nurse Howard smiled. "It sounds like you might be suffering from a little morning sickness."

"More than a little."

"I'm sorry. If you're pregnant, that's not an unusual set of symptoms, but it doesn't last forever."

"Thank God for that."

"But from now on take ibuprofen, not aspirin. You look to be in good health, Anne-Marie. Am I right?"

"Yes, I think so. I don't have much appetite lately."

"Your appetite will return, dear. Trust me. You look healthy for sure, nice and firm and athletic."

"I'm not really an athlete, unless you count cheerleading."

"I do count that," said the nurse with another smile.

Then the lab technician appeared with the test results, which he placed on Nurse Howard's desk. She studied the form for a moment or two while Anne-Marie squirmed. "Well?" she asked. "What does it say?"

"You were right. You're pregnant."

Immediately, Anne-Marie felt the knot in her stomach tighten. "I don't know what to do," she blurted out.

"It's a good sign that you're willing to admit it, which means it's good that you're here. When we aren't sure, the wisest thing we can do is ask for help."

Eleanor spoke for the first time. "Can Anne-Marie come back for additional counseling at a later date?"

"Of course. Just make an appointment. If you make the decision to carry the child to term, which it sounds like you have, you can have the best prenatal care right here in our clinic. I can't say for sure, but if you haven't had a period for two months, I'd guess you must be six or seven weeks along."

"Six or seven weeks," Anne-Marie repeated numbly.

"In which case," the nurse continued, "you'll need a thorough prenatal exam in a month or two. If we're going to have babies, we need healthy ones, as well as healthy mothers."

First she called me a woman and now she calls me a mother. It was all too, too scary. "Where would I have this exam?"

"You could have it here with us, or you could have it with your family doctor, if you prefer. I'm going to give you some literature to take home, as well as this form, which confirms you had a positive pregnancy test in our lab on today's date. You can show it to anyone or no one. That's up to you."

One of the pamphlets Nurse Howard passed across was entitled *Options in Pregnancy.* "I urge you to read through this material carefully," she said. "Hard decisions are so much harder when we don't know what our choices are."

Anne-Marie glanced at Eleanor, who was smiling. The words were nearly the same as those her big sister had used the night before.

"After you do read through your list of options and do some serious reflecting, don't hesitate to call for another appointment. We can discuss possible choices in more detail. Okay?"

"Okay," said Anne-Marie. But she was ready to leave now. "Thank you very much."

"You're welcome."

When they left the parking lot, Anne-Marie scrunched down low in her seat so she wouldn't have to look at the sign-carrying protesters. On the drive home, she leafed through the pamphlet called *Options in Pregnancy,* but wasn't able to pay close attention.

The pamphlet was divided into four distinct sections: *Parenthood, Marriage, Adoption,* and *Abortion.* That word again. She was sure that would be the ideal solution in Eleanor's mind. There were lists of specific line-items beneath each heading, but she was too anxious and upset to concentrate. She put the leaflet away in her purse.

"You're getting skinny," Eleanor observed. "What are you eating these days?"

"I don't have much appetite. I won't be skinny for long, though, will I?"

"That sounds like an attempt at humor. Do you want to talk about it?"

"Not now. Maybe later."

"Are you going to discuss it with Mom and Dad?"

"Are you kidding?" said Anne-Marie.

"Maybe you should give them a chance."

"Oh please. They wouldn't understand any of it. If they

want to help, they can give me a little freedom so I don't feel like a prisoner all the time."

Eleanor sighed before she goosed on into traffic. "They're parents, Anne-Marie. Sometimes people try to help the only way they know how."

"If you're going to be mature, you can just shut up. I don't need it right now."

"Okay, okay, my lips are sealed."

June 5

Eleanor's plane departed on time from O'Hare. Before she boarded, she gave Anne-Marie a good-bye hug at the ramp. "You make sure and follow through," she whispered.

"Okay."

"No one has to go through this alone. The counselor we talked to at Planned Parenthood can be a big help. You can trust her."

"I know," Anne-Marie agreed. "I'll talk to her again."

"And you can always call me. I gave you my new number, did you write it down?"

"I wrote it on the back of my library card."

"You have to promise," her sister persisted.

"I said I would, Eleanor, okay?" The conversation itself was out of earshot of their parents, who were standing near a vending machine. Eleanor's advice was right on target of course, but at the moment, she and Anne-Marie weren't on the same page. Anne-Marie was preoccupied with Brother Jackson and how she might be able to see him again, at least one more time. In Indiana.

Anne-Marie's appeal to her father came on the drive home. She rode in the front passenger seat, while her mother sat in the back. They were driving the Jaguar. Her father commented on the rich smell of the leather seats. Anne-Marie never knew if he loved cars for their looks or for driving.

With very little hope, she couldn't help asking her father if she could go to Indiana to attend one of Brother Jackson's tabernacle meetings.

"You're asking if you can skip a class?" her father questioned.

"No, not even. I just want to drive down there for the weekend. It wouldn't have to be the whole weekend, maybe just for the day."

"To Crawfordsville, Indiana? That's a long way." He rolled up his sleeves a turn or two and loosened his necktie.

"It's only two hours, or three at the most," Anne-Marie said. "I looked it up on the map."

Her father asked her mother if she knew anything about the situation.

"Anne-Marie and I discussed some Bible study at Sara's house the other day," she replied. "Crawfordsville is something new. I guess it's your turn now."

He didn't spend much time pondering this information. "Do you remember signing your contract?" he asked Anne-Marie.

"Of course I do." It was something she could never forget, no matter how hard she might try. The contract was a symbol of the old Anne-Marie, the girl she used to be. It was failure. "But this is on the weekend. It's not part of the contract."

Her father replied, "It's *our* part of the contract. Your mother's and mine. You're grounded, remember?"

"How could I forget?"

"Unless I'm mistaken, the contract stipulates that you won't miss any classes at all if you want to graduate or use your car on weekends."

Her father wasn't likely to be mistaken about details of this nature; he wasn't a successful attorney for no reason. She felt like telling him he was speeding, which was another form of breaking a contract. "I know what it says," she replied. "I don't even care about using the car."

"Then how would you get there?"

"I'm sure Sara Curtis would take me. Pretty sure, anyway."

"That would just be sanding off the edges, Anne-Marie. Maybe you don't understand what a contract is. A contract is binding. That means it's not something you sign, then decide later on you'll disregard the parts that may be inconvenient."

"I know what a contract is," she answered quietly.

"Maybe when we get home, you and I need to get it out and have another look at it."

"No thank you." She was glad it would never be her job to face him in court. Almost in spite of herself she said, "I was just hoping we could make an exception. Not for fun and games, but for spiritual reasons."

"Why is this weekend so important?" her father said. "Why not simply wait until summer school is over?"

"Because Brother Jackson might not be there after this weekend. There's no telling how long these crusades will stay in one place."

"Are you telling me he's leaving for some other part of the country?"

"It's possible. That's what I'm telling you." She regretted her equivocal language almost as soon as the words were out of her mouth.

Her father seized the opportunity like a treasure: "Then you don't know for certain if it's his final weekend or not."

She couldn't lie, so she admitted she couldn't be sure.

"It's possible, but not certain," her father persisted. "Is that fair to say?"

"It's fair." She sighed, wishing now that the conversation had never begun.

He seemed satisfied with that part of the agenda, so he changed the subject. "I wish I could tell you that your mother and I have been able to find some enthusiasm for this Brother Jackson character and his type of religion."

Anne-Marie didn't want a confrontation. She bit her tongue before she replied, "He's not a *character.* He's a man of God."

"He seems to be presiding over a cult of some kind."

"And what's a cult?"

Her mother leaned forward to say, "It seems like the kind of religion that doesn't have much balance."

"Balance," Anne-Marie repeated with contempt. She felt her nostrils flaring in spite of her best intentions. "Balanced religion is armchair religion."

"What does that mean?"

"It means religion without a soul. It means religion without any real commitment."

"Is that what Brother Jackson teaches?"

"It's what we learn when we become Christians."

"But we've always been Christians, Anne-Marie," said her mother. "You know that. You were baptized in the Presbyterian Church."

Anne-Marie knew there was no use in continuing this. The really significant issues of her new life with the Lord and the new life growing inside her were beyond the range of her parents' comprehension. Or her own. Besides, she had another headache.

She understood now that surrendering in this situation was good. It was simply another dimension—even if a painful one—of the pattern of submission Jesus wanted from her. It was taught in the Word; it meant losing herself to find herself. Arguing wouldn't work.

June 8

Friday morning, her mother helped her with an English essay. From her desk, Anne-Marie could see her father using rubbing compound on the left front fender of the Beamer. And he was dressed for an appearance in court. *If he could only understand as much about the Lord as he does about restoring cars,* she thought.

"Pay attention," her mother urged. "Your mind is wandering."

It was true. She was bad enough at concentration under normal conditions, but conditions in her life right now were in turmoil. Her mother looking over her shoulder at this point didn't help. "I can do this, Mother, okay?"

"Okay, so show me. Show me you know how to cut that paragraph and paste it on page two."

Anne-Marie could feel her shoulders slump. She didn't know. "You know I have problems with stuff on the Edit bar."

"Okay, then, let me help you."

"Why are you doing this?"

"Why? Because I want to help. Do you think your father and I want you to fail?"

"Mother, I'm on a contract. It's like being behind bars. It's like totally humiliating."

"It's more like being on probation, but the point is that the contract is something we worked out with the school to help you succeed. Now pay attention." Anne-Marie watched somewhat numbly as her mother dropped the Edit bar on the monitor and showed her the procedure for cutting and pasting. "Now you try it."

Anne-Marie manipulated the process successfully a time or two before her mother said, "I have to go to work. If you have any other questions about it, you can ask me this evening. I'll try to help."

"You know, this is ironic," said Anne-Marie. "In most houses it's the teenagers who have to teach their parents about computers."

"Ironic is a good word for it," said her mother before leaving the room. "And you need to start eating more. You're getting too thin."

"I know. I will."

As soon as her mother was gone, Anne-Marie set to work on editing her essay. Her topic was a local drug program called Project Oz and the services it provided for teenagers. She could call Richard and quiz him, if she wanted; he had been in the program once or twice during sophomore year. But that wouldn't work, because any call from her would only encourage him to try to start up their relationship again.

The topic of drugs reminded her of the consultation with Nurse Howard, which reminded her she was pregnant without an option. This reminded her how queasy her stomach was, too much so for eating, and before she knew it there were tears running down her face while she found herself staring at the stars and bars on the screen saver.

Anne-Marie stood up so she could pace. Looking out her window, she could see that her mother's car was gone, as well as her father's. The Planned Parenthood pamphlet *Am I Parent Material?* was in her desk drawer, hidden beneath some of Eleanor's academic awards and certificates. She took it out and laid it right next to her keyboard. The pamphlet seemed like it was a living entity, with eyes that could track her movement in any part of the room. She didn't know what to do and Eleanor was gone. She took the library card from her wallet and stared at Eleanor's phone number on the back.

If she went back to that clinic, she'd have to go alone. Anne-Marie suddenly felt a level of anxiety and desperation far more acute than any she'd ever known. She felt tears coming again, and she wished like anything she had a cigarette. It would fit perfectly with this restless pattern of nervous pacing.

At that moment the doorbell rang. She wiped her eyes quickly with tissue before she went downstairs to see who was there.

It was a young man with short hair dressed in a dark suit and tie. A young woman was with him; she wore a print dress which reached to midcalf. The young man introduced himself as Jacob, the young woman as Gloria; they were both holding Bibles.

As she shook their hands, Anne-Marie recognized their faces from Brother Jackson's tabernacle meeting. "What d'you want?" she asked.

Jacob came right to the point. "We saw you make a visit to the Planned Parenthood clinic."

"You saw that?"

"We monitor there sometimes. Please don't be offended, but we feel it's a part of what the Lord is calling us to do."

Anne-Marie's first thought was, *Someone's been watching me.* "I only went there because my sister thought it might be a good idea. How did you find my house?"

Gloria smiled and said, "We try to maintain a networking system to help the convicted. We hope and pray you would never consider having an abortion," she added.

It never occurred to Anne-Marie that these two people might be invading her privacy. "I could never have an abortion. God could never forgive a thing like that."

"Praise Him for that," said Gloria.

"Praise Him," echoed Jacob.

Gloria continued, "Remember, if you're pregnant, what's growing inside you is a living child with an eternal soul. It isn't just tissue, to be scraped away, like they try to tell you."

Anne-Marie suddenly felt embarrassed she'd ever gone there, or did the embarrassment result from the fact she'd been caught? "I could never have an abortion," she repeated. "We just talked to a counselor who gave us literature and told us about eating right and health habits and things like that."

"That's the pattern their seduction usually takes," said Jacob.

"Did this counselor ask you to return another time?" Gloria asked her.

"Well, yes, she said I could come back later and talk about all my options. She said I could have a prenatal exam in their clinic."

"That's their usual pattern of deception," Jacob said. "They soften you up as if all they want to do is give you parenting advice, and then when they get you back they lead you in the direction of the abortion option."

"They can make it seem like it's your choice, and not theirs," said Gloria. "They do it again and again to confused young women. They're very good at it."

Anne-Marie was scared. Her visit with Nurse Howard hadn't seemed like this kind of prelude, but she did know from fellowshipping with enough believers that the abortion people were very clever.

Gloria took Anne-Marie's hand. "Would you like to pray about this, dear?"

"Yes, I would," Anne-Marie found herself answering quickly.

The three of them went to their knees right there in the entryway. Gloria kept a tight grip on her hand. "Lord Jesus," she began, with her eyes squeezed tightly shut, "we just give you all the praise and glory."

"All the honor," added Jacob.

Gloria continued her prayer, "Father, we just ask your blessing on our sister Anne-Marie right now, at this very moment."

"We ask you to be right by her side, Jesus," added Jacob, "in the days ahead and fill her heart with your loving presence. We ask you, lead her in the direction of all right and true decisions, and bless her with your guidance every step of the way."

"Dear Jesus, don't let her be seduced by the Evil One," prayed Gloria, "whatever clever form he might take. We pray you just spread your whole armor to protect her every step of the way from those who would lead her astray and into sin."

Anne-Marie felt a sudden loosening of the fearful knot in her stomach. *I didn't put enough trust in the Lord to begin with,* she thought. *What made me think there could be answers in contracts with a high school or visits to a counselor at Planned Parenthood? Why wasn't my faith stronger, why did it take two strangers to seek me out and lead me to the Lord's exclusive guidance?* The tears which rolled down her cheeks were new ones, different ones, tears of joy and relief.

As the three of them got slowly to their feet, Anne-

Marie brushed away her tears with the back of her hand. "I want to thank you for coming," she said truthfully. "Praise Him."

"Praise Jesus, Sister," said Jacob. "You can call on us anytime you feel the need. Here's my card." He handed her a calling card with his name, address, and phone number.

"Put all your faith in the Lord," advised Gloria as they were leaving, "and He will fulfill your every need." Then they left.

Put your faith in the Lord, and He will fulfill your every need, she repeated to herself as she showered down her tears in a good, cleansing cry. *If my faith was stronger, I would have known sooner.*

June 9

When Anne-Marie decided, it was Richard she called on for help. Not that she wanted to, but who else was there? Brooke would only try to talk her out of it. Chris Weems would probably take her, but he was really stressed, if the stories Brooke was telling were true. Which they probably were; Brooke could be a self-centered prima donna, but she wasn't a liar. Besides, how could she talk to Chris Weems? As strung out as she herself was, how could she listen to his problems? She would pray for him.

Sara Curtis would probably be willing to take her, but Anne-Marie wouldn't know how to talk to her about being pregnant. Besides, Sara would probably be so scandalized she would drive off the road into a ditch.

So it was Richard or nobody, as far as Anne-Marie could see. She called him to ask him to drive her to Crawfordsville, Indiana.

"Cool."

"It's not what you think," she said quickly.

"What do I think?"

"This is not like a date or anything, I just need a ride to Crawfordsville. I want you to drop me off and then come back."

"Why?"

It took a few seconds to gather herself. It was hard enough just taking off like this, without the added strain of trying to come up with explanations. Anne-Marie finally said, "I'm pregnant."

"You're pregnant?"

"That's what I said. I'm going to have a baby."

"Jesus."

"It's not your baby, Richard. Don't worry."

"Be still my heart."

"I said you're not the father. Don't worry. All I'm asking you to do is give me the ride and drop me off."

"Why do you want to go to Crawfordsville?"

"Because that's where the father is. I've got to see him."

There was a brief silence on the other end before Richard said, "Does the guy know?"

Anne-Marie took a deep breath, followed by another. "No. He doesn't know. Now please stop asking me so many questions. Don't you know how hard this is for me?"

"Hey. You want me to do you this favor, which is pretty weird by the way, so you might have to deal with some questions. Okay?"

"Okay. What else do you want to know?"

"What about your folks?"

"They're not here. They're at a wedding reception in

Rockford. They won't be back home until like midnight or something."

"All those cars at your house, and you want me to give you a ride? What's up with that?"

"I couldn't do that. I might not be coming back, and I just couldn't do that to my dad. I couldn't just take one of his cars and abandon it somewhere."

"You might not be comin' back? This gets better and better. But you want to go right away, that's what you're sayin', isn't it?"

As crazy as it sounded, she could only answer, "Yes. Within the next half hour maybe. I've got a bag packed."

"This is so nuts I almost have to like it. You're sure I'm not the father."

"Totally. Don't even think about it."

She could tell Richard was lighting up. Even over the phone, she could hear the click of his lighter.

Quickly, she relented on the car issue. "Okay, we'll drive one of my dad's cars. But if you end up dropping me off, you have to promise to bring it straight back home."

Apparently, Richard had heard enough. "What are we drivin', Anne-Marie?"

"We can take the Beamer."

"Cool. I'll be there."

The black BMW purred like a kitten. Richard said so. Anne-Marie couldn't care less what sound it made. The uncertainty of her future roiled in her stomach like a whirlpool.

Richard was driving south on Highway 1, a secondary two-lane that went right through a succession of small towns. Anne-Marie wondered why he didn't want to take the interstate.

"Too many cops," was Richard's answer. "We need to open this baby up from time to time. There are lots of curves on this road, and some of them are fairly tight. BMWs are famous for cornering."

"Whatever. Just have it back by eight o'clock, or nine at the latest."

"No problem. Plenty of time."

"You have to promise."

Richard lit a cigarette before he answered. "I think I just did. Where d'you want me to put the keys?"

"Just lock the car and leave the keys in the mailbox. That's probably the best way." She had this urge to tell him her father didn't allow smoking in this car—or any of his cars for that matter—but it didn't seem very important right now.

"You're losing weight, you know that?"

"Not you, too," she said. She reminded herself that she wasn't running *away*, she was running *to*. By going to Brother Jackson, she was seeking the shelter which only the Lord could provide.

"How come you're losing weight? If you're pregnant, you should be gaining weight, right?"

"You sound like my mother. It's just my sick stomach and no appetite. It's called morning sickness."

"Have you told your folks you're pregnant?"

"Oh please, Richard. How could I do that? I'm on a contract, I didn't even get to graduate with the class. I should like add this into the mix?"

Richard didn't answer right away. "I hate to say it, Anne-Marie, but wouldn't you be better off getting your diploma in summer school than running off with this guy?"

"He's not a *guy*. And you're the last person I know who should be giving lectures on responsible behavior. And I'm not even sure I'll be running off with him, as you put it."

"Okay, sorry."

"And I really wish you wouldn't make me talk to you this way."

"I can't make you do anything, Anne-Marie."

She got the point. "Just lighten up, okay? This is all hard enough without the second-guessing. Besides, I thought if you got to drive this car it would keep you occupied."

They were reaching speeds of up to 100 miles per hour between the little villages.

There would be reconciliations, she kept reminding herself. With her parents, with her friends, with Eleanor. Most of all, with her Lord and Savior. Withdrawing to Brother Jackson didn't mean she was closing all the doors in her life.

She said to Richard, "Let me have one of your cigarettes?"

Richard fished one out of his pocket and gave it to her. He helped her light it before he said, "You wanna be careful now; you're smoking for two, remember?"

This was as adult as Richard Bone could be. Anne-Marie suddenly appreciated him. If she had to be chauffeured to this uncertain destiny, she was glad he was the driver.

She inhaled deeply two times before she felt the intoxicating rush in her brain. Maybe it was just not having one for so long. It was euphoric, though. "You didn't put anything in this, did you?"

"Put anything in?"

"You know, like weed or something? You didn't crumble up a little grass in here like you used to do?"

"Would I do a thing like that?"

"Remember who you're talking to. I've seen you do it before." Then she didn't want to talk anymore. She closed her eyes.

They were in Crawfordsville in a little over two hours. Richard said his only regret was that the road was straighter than he'd hoped. "I think I'll go back a different way."

"It's up to you. Just make sure you leave the car the way I told you."

"We've covered that, huh? You're sure you want me to leave you here? That's your final answer?"

She ignored the humor. "Yes, I've made up my mind. I either have the courage to go with my convictions or I don't."

"And you're sure you'll find this guy?"

"I'm sure. And don't be late getting the car back." Then she added, "Please."

"Like I said." They were parked in a city park with a large gazebo and several small picnic shelters. It wasn't hard to know where the tabernacle meetings were being held. The signs were everywhere. The fairgrounds were visible from the park, even though at quite a distance.

She plopped her bag on one of the tables in a shelter. "You travel light," said Richard.

"Yes."

"Traveling light is always best."

"I'm glad you think so." Anne-Marie felt light in the head, too, but her nerves were calmer.

"You're sure you know what you're doing."

"As sure as I can be, Richard."

"I hope you're gonna be okay, huh?"

"Please go now. I'll be better than okay. I'm not alone." She almost said, *You can pray for me if you want*, but she knew it wouldn't work with him.

He didn't answer right away. She guessed he was avoiding any negative remarks about her new religious beliefs. "I'll tell you what," he finally said. "If you run into any problems, you can call me, okay?"

Anne-Marie didn't look up at him. She did have her cell phone with her. She was running her thumbnail along a soft groove in the surface of the picnic table. "Thanks. And thanks for bringing me. But just go now, okay?"

She watched him go. She watched the Beamer all the way down the street until it passed some downtown stores, went through a traffic signal, and then disappeared. Even though it was just Richard, she felt alone.

It was after dark when she finally got to speak to Brother Jackson. She'd waited more than an hour by a fence near an open fairground building which served as the site for the praise meeting. When the final amens were concluded, and the last people finished speaking to him in private, Anne-Marie approached him. They spoke alone next to a livestock building that had lots of goats and a few sheep.

Anne-Marie couldn't help seeing it as a sign: the first fellowship message she'd ever heard him deliver was the one about keeping company with the sheep. She was bold by seeking company with the sheep, not the goats like Planned Parenthood and school counselors who drafted prison-sentence contracts. She found herself inhaling deeply; the agricultural smell was deep and rich.

The surprise on Brother Jackson's face was genuine, but so was the pleasure. Her heart leaped up.

Naturally, he was caught off guard when she told him she was pregnant.

"Are you sure?" he asked.

"Yes. I'm sure."

"Are you sure it's mine?" he wanted to know.

It was a question which hurt, but she simply answered yes again. The lighting where they stood was dim, dim enough she hoped he wouldn't be able to see the disappointment in her eyes.

"What should we do?" he asked her. "What d'you want to do?"

"I don't know," Anne-Marie answered truthfully. "I was hoping you might know."

"We would need the Lord's guidance, but I don't have

the time right now. I'm on my way to Oklahoma for a crusade not far from Stillwater."

"When are you going?"

"Right away." Brother Jackson was looking at the large tote bag resting on the ground beside her feet. "Do you have things packed?"

"A few things."

"But why, Sister?"

"I'm not exactly sure." How embarrassing was this? "I knew you were leaving Crawfordsville to go someplace else. Maybe I thought you might take me with you. Maybe some part of me was hoping it could happen that way."

"To Oklahoma? Oh, Sister Anne-Marie, I'm not in a position to take anyone with me, not starting out on a new crusade."

But I'm not just anyone, she wanted to say. "This is our baby, though."

"Praise God for the miracle of it, but we need His help to find our way out of the darkness. We don't know what to do."

"I can't go home, though, I just can't."

"You can't go home?"

"Not to my parents. They don't understand anything of the new person I am. They can't understand."

"I'm with you," said Brother Jackson. He bit his lip before pushing some hair out of his eyes. "I could take you to Camp Shaddai," he finally said.

What's that? she asked herself. But she did feel a flicker of hope because it sounded like he had a plan. "What's Camp Shaddai?"

"It's a spiritual retreat center where I've worked from time to time. It's down in southern Illinois."

Southern Illinois seemed awfully far away. Maybe as far as 300 miles or more. "Is it a Spirit-filled place?"

For the first time, Brother Jackson smiled his glorious smile. "The Holy Spirit dwells there as surely as the cottonwood trees grow and the frogs twang along the shore. It's a place to be alone with the Lord and wait upon His guidance. I can even introduce you to Sister Abigail."

"Who's Sister Abigail?"

"You can trust her to help you search for direction. You couldn't be in better hands."

"Let's go then," she beseeched him. She had never seen the place, nor met Sister Abigail, but it felt like hope; she needed to grab it.

"I can't think of a better plan," he said. "Both of us will be alone to think. Both of us will be in a place where we can wait upon the Lord without outside distractions."

"Will you be there, too?" Anne-Marie asked hopefully.

"No, I'll be in Oklahoma. For only a couple of weeks, though."

"Only for two weeks?"

"Three at the most. Can you trust me?"

"And then we'll be together and we'll know what we should do?"

"We will, with the Lord's help."

"Sister Abigail will be there though?"

"She will be there. You couldn't be in better hands."

Hadn't he said that once already? Without further hesitation, though, Anne-Marie picked up her bag. She followed Brother Jackson as he led the way to his car, an old Chrysler with plenty of body rust and a crumpled front fender. He told her to put the bag in the backseat. As soon as she tossed it in, he said, "This takes courage, Sister."

Her spirits rose again. This new plan of action seemed to fill her with growing confidence. It was freedom from her parents in any case, and from the humiliating lockdown of the contract. "It either takes courage or faith," she replied. "Maybe when my faith is strong enough, I won't need to worry about things like courage. That's what I pray for."

"Praise God for your trust and submission, Sister. Hop in, then. It won't take me but a few minutes to get my things together. I travel light, too."

Brother Jackson drove fast in the old Chrysler. Not as fast as Richard had driven the Beamer, of course, that wouldn't be possible. The car windows were open, so it wasn't easy to carry on a conversation. She didn't mind; she was free. She watched as the green exit signs flew by, one by one, until, physically and mentally exhausted, she fell asleep.

She didn't awake until they reached the urban bypass that skirted the city of Springfield, Illinois. Traffic was practically nonexistent, but the streetlights were bright. Brother

Jackson had found a country/Christian radio station which came in clearly, although most of his earlier attempts had been undermined by fading and static. A lovely song was on: Someone had combined the old James Taylor song "You've Got a Friend" with the Christian hymn "What a Friend We Have in Jesus." Anne-Marie found herself humming along.

Once past Springfield, she fell asleep again. The next time she awoke, Brother Jackson was pulling into a rest stop. "We're just south of a town called Litchfield," he told her. "I'm afraid I'm exhausted, Sister Anne-Marie. We're going to have to bed down for the night." Saying this, he pulled the car to the remote end of the parking area. Anne-Marie knew when he said *bed down* he didn't mean they'd be sleeping together.

There were only two or three other cars in view, and the parking lot lights didn't cast far in this direction. Brother Jackson got out to rummage in the trunk until he found the sleeping bag he was looking for, and a pillow. "You can sleep in the car," he told her. "I'll just stretch out on one of those picnic tables over there in that shelter."

"But that won't be comfortable at all," said Anne-Marie.

"Don't you worry about that. This old sleeping bag and I have made do in a hundred worse places than this. Much worse. I'll see you in the morning, Sister. God bless."

"God bless," she returned.

When he was gone, she found she was grateful. If they had stayed in a motel, she would have been tempted again. It was so odd how she knew him intimately but really didn't know him much at all. She knew his body and a few of his favorite sermon themes.

Other than the time they had made love, she had only spoken to him briefly once or twice. Besides listening to him preach, of course. But listening to a person giving a sermon wasn't the same thing as personal sharing.

She curled up in the backseat of the car. She might have been sleepier if she hadn't taken those long naps earlier along the way.

She couldn't help thinking back to the time she'd spent the night with Richard at the lake in the backseat of the old Chevy. This situation was much different, but there were similarities, too.

By the time they'd gotten to the lake, they'd finished off two six-packs of wine coolers and were drunk as lords. Richard took the curved spillway at about seventy miles an hour, just to see how the Chevy performed. When they'd started skidding a little bit, he let up. They found a private parking space off the shoulder of a small access road.

Richard had lit up two of his "tailor-made joints," as he called them, and given one to her. "How do you make these things?" she'd asked him.

"Simple. You take about half of the tobacco out of the end of a Marlboro, then fill the empty space with reefer. That way none of the grass gets wasted."

The explanation had made her giddy. She began to giggle uncontrollably.

"What's so funny?" he'd asked, taking a long drag and holding it.

Her answer had come between her bouts of the giggles. "It doesn't sound simple at all. I'm just like trying to picture you bent over like some watchmaker using tweezers to move tobacco and marijuana back and forth." She laughed out loud.

"You're drunk," he said.

"Yeah, so? What about you?"

"It's not a procedure like using an eyeglass at a workbench. Most of these I fixed during play practice this afternoon."

"How did you have the time?" she'd asked.

"They were rehearsing their lines for this one-act that Chris Weems wrote. I'm in the other two, but not that one. I had plenty of time." He had lifted her skirt to her waist by this time.

"What play did Chris Weems write?"

Richard had laughed. "It's called *Changing of the Guard.* I can't tell you how lame it is."

She was already drunk, and by now she'd finished her doctored cigarette and was high and disoriented, like she was flying. She'd wanted Richard to take her, but she was curious about Chris's play at the same time. In her mind-altered state, she couldn't seem to separate the one activity from the other. She went into gales of laughter before she managed to ask, "What is his play like?"

"Who cares?"

"I'm just curious."

By this time he had begun tugging at her underwear but seemed annoyed. "Are you ready for this or what?" he wanted to know.

She was still giggling. "I'm ready. I'm almost ready. Just tell me about the play and then I'll be totally ready. Have you got a condom?"

"Yeah, I've got a condom. And okay, if you have to know, here's how it goes. There's this guy who finds out he's gay."

"In the play, you mean?"

"No, on *Judge Judy.* Of course I mean the play."

"And like how old is he?"

"What difference does it make?"

"How old is he?"

"He's out of school, so I guess he's an adult. A young one. Let's say he's twenty-three, okay?"

"Okay," she had laughed. "Twenty-three, then. So he finds out he's gay, what's the problem?"

"The problem is he wants to change. He figures the best way is to take out all the beautiful women he can find, hoping he'll get hooked by one. Then the problem is, none of the women he asks will go out with him. It's supposed to be funny. There. Are you satisfied?"

She'd still been giggling, even while he worked the condom into place. After they'd made love, he was still irritable. "You weren't even into that. You just went through the motions, like sleepwalking through a play."

"I'm sorry," she'd said. "You're right. But with all that wine cooler and then the grass, I feel like I'm just tripping."

"Whatever happened to passion?" he asked. "The whole world doesn't have any passion anymore."

"I don't know. I guess it's just gone with the wine." And she began to laugh again.

They'd fallen asleep in the backseat and didn't recover until after sunrise.

When she finally got back home she was grounded for two weeks. And her father had had a few choice words for Richard, too: "I want you to stay away from Anne-Marie," he said. "You're a resourceful, slick guy, you shouldn't have too much trouble finding another girl."

"But Dad—"

"But nothing. You've got plenty of problems to deal with without adding a risky lifestyle into the mix. That's it. Case closed."

Richard had apologized several times before he left.

It was about three weeks later that her mother had shown her the *Tribune* articles on the problems of the overpopulation of Canada geese in the northwest suburbs.

June 10

By the time she awoke, the sky was bright and birds were singing, though it was still early morning. She might have slept longer but for the fact she had to pee so bad. For the first time in days, maybe weeks, she felt refreshed.

Anne-Marie approached the picnic table where Brother Jackson had spent the night. She discovered him reading from the Bible and talking with a middle-aged woman. It wasn't the time to interrupt. He took his ministry so naturally into every nook and cranny of the world. He was always about the Lord's work.

So instead, she fetched her backpack from the car and headed for the convenience center, which was a modern limestone building with clean rest rooms and an information counter with maps and pamphlets for tourists. In the bathroom, she scrubbed with soap, using paper towels from the dispenser to dry herself.

She changed her T-shirt after applying underarm deodorant. She had stubble, which reminded her that she hadn't thought to pack a razor. Her bra was dirty, so she took it off. She didn't have another one, but there would be laundry facilities at Camp Shaddai. Since she didn't want to appear provocative, she chose her Chicago Bulls shirt, which was double extra large and long enough to reach her hips.

Anne-Marie felt a sudden wave of guilt while brushing her teeth. Her parents would be worried sick. She didn't want them to suffer; they weren't really bad parents, they just couldn't understand what it meant to have the Lord as the true center of your life.

She wanted to be free, but didn't want them to suffer. If there was a way to reassure them, she wanted to find it. She could call Eleanor. Her purse was inside the backpack, with the library card and Eleanor's new number in Cambridge, Massachusetts.

Near the counter in the welcome center were several pay phones against the wall. Anne-Marie had plenty of change. She decided to use one of the phones instead of her cell. It wasn't yet eight A.M. even on the East Coast, but Eleanor was awake. As succinctly as she could, Anne-Marie summarized yesterday's decision and her current flight with Brother Jackson.

"Oh Anne-Marie, you can't be serious."

"I am, though. And I'm perfectly safe. That's the first thing I want you to know, that I'm not at any risk." *Except as a student,* she thought; *I've always been an at-risk student.*

"Where are you going?"

"We're on our way to a spiritual retreat center. It's a place where I can get away from everything and pray about my problems and what to do."

"Where is this retreat center?"

Anne-Marie felt a little foolish when she had to admit, "All I know for sure is, it's someplace in southern Illinois."

"Where are you now?" Eleanor demanded.

"We're at a rest stop somewhere on the interstate. I'm not exactly sure where. The point I'm trying to make is that I'm safe."

"You're safe with your evangelist, is that what you're telling me?"

"Brother Jackson. Yes, I'm safe with him."

"You're breaking your contract then, aren't you?"

"Don't even go there, Eleanor. That's not why I called you. I can get that from Mom and Dad or any counselor at the high school."

"I'm sorry," said Eleanor, after a brief pause. "What can I do for you?"

"You can call Mom and Dad. Just call them and tell them I'm okay."

"How do I know you're okay?"

"Because I'm telling you the truth. Just trust me. I called, didn't I? All I want is just the one favor, okay?"

"I don't like it, but I'll probably do it," her big sister admitted. "I don't want Mom and Dad worried sick."

"Neither do I. Thanks, Eleanor. Thanks a lot."

"I'm not finished yet, Anne-Marie. I don't want me worried sick, either. When you get to this retreat center, I want you to call me again. Reverse the charges if you have to, but call me."

"Okay."

"You have to promise."

"I promise."

"And while I've got you on the line," Eleanor continued, "what about Nurse Howard? What about the counseling center and your options?"

"I haven't forgotten about it," said Anne-Marie quickly. Although after the visit she'd received from Jacob and Gloria, she'd forgotten about it in any way that mattered. "I'm only going to a place where I can be free to meditate and pray. I have to know the Lord's will."

"You'd better be telling me the truth. It's a big favor you're asking me to do. I don't even know where you'll be."

"I'd like to tell you the name of the place, but Mom and Dad would pull it out of you. Then they'd come get me and bring me back. I'm not eighteen yet—I don't have any rights. You don't know what it's like to be under everybody else's rules all the time."

"You think I was never seventeen?"

"You were never on academic probation or receiving progress reports in the mail or under a performance contract. You want to argue with that?"

"No, I'm not going to argue that point. All I can say is, I'll keep my promise and I expect you to keep yours."

"I will, Eleanor, you can trust me. And thanks. Thanks a lot."

"You're welcome. I guess. Stay well and keep safe."

"Okay, bye."

Anne-Marie felt relieved. She stowed her gear in the trunk of the car just as Brother Jackson announced that he was ready for the road. "I called Sister Abigail at Camp Shaddai before you were awake," he told her. "She'll be ready for us this afternoon, so everything seems to be falling into place."

Anne-Marie decided not to say anything about her own phone call. "That's the way it works when you put your trust in the Lord, huh?"

"Sister, I couldn't say it better."

Since they were both famished, they stopped at the first McDonald's they could spot from the highway. Not only was she hungry, Anne-Marie was grateful for the rest room opportunity. She had the Egg McMuffin with a side of hash browns. Brother Jackson chose the Big Breakfast with pancakes and sausage. He insisted on paying.

"But I have some money," Anne-Marie reminded him.

"Put your money away; this is on me."

It was the best appetite she could remember having for weeks. The breakfast sandwich tasted delicious. Anne-Marie felt her sense of freedom dovetailing with her sense of destiny.

Even with her mouth partly full, she needed to tell him, "I remember the night I became a Christian."

"Praise God. Let's hear it."

"It was the first night I heard you preach. I know you don't like that word, though; it was that night at the tabernacle. I felt the Spirit of the Lord come all over me like a heavenly poncho. I felt such a relief from my sins."

"And were you a sinner?"

"I'd have to say so," she admitted, avoiding his eyes. "When I was a cheerleader, we used to smoke pot behind the bleachers at halftime. I was guilty of fornication, too." It seemed so effortless to share intimate information with him.

"All your sins are forgiven, though, the minute you lay them at the throne. You know that, don't you, Anne-Marie?"

"I know it now. I was also guilty of the sin of laziness, especially when it came to school. I never worked up to my ability. I didn't even graduate on time. If I'm going to graduate, it will have to be through summer school, making up for low grades. About the only good thing is, I've been reading my Bible a lot."

"Praise Jesus," said Brother quickly. Then he declared, "I never graduated high school myself, but I can honestly say that due to the Lord's guidance, it's never been a problem."

Anne-Marie was surprised but also encouraged. "Anyway," she repeated herself, "I first knew the Lord at the end of that praise meeting."

"Praise Him all the more then," said Brother Jackson.

"Praise the fact that He still chooses me as a vehicle for the coming of His Kingdom."

"Can you remember when it was that you became a Christian?"

"Yes indeed, Sister. It was in an oil field, of all places." He was very good at forking large amounts of food into his mouth and chewing on one side but speaking distinctly at the same time.

"An oil field?"

"Yes, but I'm getting ahead of myself." He flashed the winning smile. "I grew up down around Fayetteville, Arkansas. We were as poor as we could be. My daddy reenlisted in the navy and went somewhere overseas. He wasn't too good at writing letters or sending money, so we pretty much lost touch with him."

"Oh, that's too bad."

"It seemed bad at the time. Anyway, I dropped out of high school and went to work for a grain company, shoveling corn out of bins and into processing chambers. I had to lie about my age to get the job, but we needed the money.

"My only religion came from this colored church we used to go to when I was real young. I can remember singing old Negro spirituals while I was shoveling away at the grain elevator. It helped pass the time. My momma was working as a housekeeper at a local motel, so we were pretty much poor most of the time."

Anne-Marie felt embarrassed just thinking about all the

money and resources that had blessed her own life. She could see Brother Jackson had lived a hard life, but it wasn't surprising to her. Maybe that was part of the reason he'd developed such strong moral character.

He said he needed a refill on his coffee and asked her if he could get her anything. "No thanks," she answered. "I'm good."

When he got back, he continued the story. "After Momma died, I left Arkansas and drove a truck awhile for a gravel company. Then they went out of business, so the next thing I knew, I found myself in Texas, working in an oil field. It was real hard work, and real dirty, but the money was good."

Finished with his breakfast, Brother Jackson was wiping his mouth with a napkin. He sipped a little of his coffee before he said, "Anyway, there was this one day when I was up the chute on this oil rig, and a big storm was coming. Lightning and thunder like you wouldn't believe. You'd of thought Armageddon was right up the street.

"I'd been changing out of my clothes, didn't even have my shoes on. They told me to climb up the rigging real fast and cap off a couple of outlets before the storm hit. Well, I didn't make it. I was screwing on one of the caps as fast as I could when lightning hit the rig. I'll never forget the sound it made, about like a rifle shot, or the smell, either. It was the smell of burning metal, like an industrial fire."

"Were you hurt?"

He shook his head. "I was not hurt. Not a scratch on

me. Two of the other workers were hit direct, though, and didn't survive. God rest their souls. But I had the shakes. I can remember just shaking in place, paralyzed with fear. The rig was on fire, it was raining cats and dogs, and the two fallen workers were down there on the ground. And then I saw my shoes. They were just construction shoes, work boots you might call them. Laying on the ground just as peaceful as they could be."

"Why did you pay attention to the shoes?"

"All of a sudden my shoes were like my sign from the Lord. There was the fire from the rig which was burning around me right there in the rain and the shoes on the ground. And I was suddenly all at peace. In my mind was the story of Moses and the burning bush. 'Take off your shoes, Moses, for you are standing on hallowed ground.' It was that very moment when I knew the Lord was calling me to be His messenger. One of His messengers, anyway. So that's a long story, Sister, but it's the answer to your question. That was the precise moment when the Lord set me on the path and I've been on it ever since."

"So did you go to seminary, then? Is that how you became a preacher?"

"Not what most people would call a seminary, not a formal one. I took a job in a convenience store in Lubbock, Texas, so I could have my nights free for Bible school. It was a school where they taught the Word. That's what the Lord longs for most—people to preach the Word."

Hearing the words *convenience store* gave Anne-Marie a brief lump in her throat. Would her picture be plastered in places like that as a missing person? Would there be an 800 number to call? She forced herself not to think about it.

"Most mainstream seminaries," Brother Jackson went on, "are too mixed up with church financing and committees and other extraneous activities. They get so bogged down in the details of running a business, and politics, they forget that the real goal is the preaching of the Word."

Anne-Marie knew how right he was. She remembered the numerous occasions of Presbyterian pettiness reported by her parents. It was more like being on committees or school boards than a sincere effort to seek the Lord.

As soon as Brother Jackson finished his coffee, they were on the road again.

It was almost noon by the time Brother Jackson found his way to the winding gravel road that snaked its way through timber and limestone bluffs. Anne-Marie found it hard to believe they were still in Illinois; it looked more like the Missouri Ozarks. Not only was the scenery breathtaking, it was also safely removed from the world. If Sister Abigail was half as spiritual as Brother Jackson claimed she was, it would be a refuge from all fears and problems.

"It's so beautiful," she said.

"No argument there," Brother Jackson agreed. And then he smiled. " 'The earth is the Lord's and the fulness thereof.' "

Anne-Marie saw occasional backpacking hikers on rugged trails. She asked him if they were almost there yet.

"Just about. Can't be more than a mile or two now."

When they did reach the entrance to the camp, they passed beneath a rustic wooden archway with a huge timber across and the words *Camp Shaddai* formed from equally rustic wooden letters. A tarmac parking lot was located near a low-slung log-cabin-style central dining hall. There were several pine trees nearby, as well as sweet gum and flourishing patches of sumac. Anne-Marie was comforted by the beauty and serenity.

Brother Jackson led her along a narrow blacktop path to the quarters where he assured her she would be allowed to stay. Sister Abigail was waiting to greet them at the door of her residential unit, a larger bungalow in the same log cabin tradition, but with a long addition connected to the near side of the creek. She greeted Anne-Marie warmly, taking her hand in both of her own.

Anne-Marie decided immediately that she had never seen a woman so beautiful. Her makeup was applied expertly. Her clear skin was richly tanned. She wore her hair in a stylish, well-formed blond blunt cut. Abigail had fine features and regular, very white teeth. "We're so happy to have you here, Anne-Marie," said Sister Abigail. "You'll find the Spirit alive and well here at Shaddai. We pray that the comfort and guidance you seek will be made known to you."

Comfort and guidance? What details had Brother Jackson

shared with her on the phone? But Anne-Marie merely said, "Thank you. Thanks a lot for letting me stay with you."

"You are welcome. Are these the only things you've brought with you?"

Anne-Marie was carrying only the backpack and tote bag. "This is it. I figure it's best to travel light." Then she laughed nervously.

Sister Abigail and Brother Jackson laughed as well. Abigail was wearing a collared white shirt with delicate embroidery to define the seams, and a series of seemingly random lines sewn on the front. If you stared at the lines long enough, though, you could see how they formed the word *Jesus* by means of an optical trick.

"Let me show you around," said the counselor. "You'll want to know where your bed is in the dorm, and you'll need a place to unpack your things."

"Sure."

"Afterwards, maybe I can give you a tour of some of our other facilities. At least the ones that are close."

"Sure," Anne-Marie repeated with enthusiasm. It disappointed her to see, though, that Brother Jackson did not intend to join them. "You're not coming?"

"Not now, Sister. I need to keep moving. It's hundreds of miles to Oklahoma, and the Lord wants me there the day after tomorrow."

"You mean you're leaving right away, without any lunch or anything?"

"I guess I feel like there's no choice." He was smiling broadly. He put his arm around her shoulders.

"Is it okay if I walk you to your car?" she asked.

"I surely wish you would. Come on, then." They headed back the way they came. He urged her to seek the Lord and all His wisdom while they were apart.

"You're coming back though, right?"

"Of course I'm coming back. Just as soon as the Oklahoma crusade is finished."

"So how long will that be?" The security that Sister Abigail brought took a dip when Anne-Marie thought of Brother Jackson so far away.

"Two or three weeks most likely," was his answer. "If it lasts longer than that, it means we're having unusual success. Praise Him for that, if it happens."

"Praise the Lord," Anne-Marie repeated, trying to set aside all selfish feelings.

They were at the car. When Brother hugged her goodbye, it was not a hug lovers would share, but a friendly one, a quick peck on one cheek and then the other. " 'The Lord is with you,' " he whispered quietly. " 'If God is with you, who can be against you?' " And then he was gone.

June 10

Anne-Marie watched the rattletrap Chrysler as it scattered some dust just before disappearing around the bend. It was an old and junky car, so different from the BMW she had watched fade from view in Indiana. But then, Brother Jackson was not a prisoner of material things. He would be back; Anne-Marie knew it.

The first thing Sister Abigail showed her was the dorm. It was a long narrow room, with a smooth and shiny concrete floor painted gray. There were eight twin beds, approximately six feet apart, lined regularly on each side of the room. Sister Abigail said two of them were unoccupied, so Anne-Marie asked if she could have the one closer to the bathroom. If she was going to have to pee so much, it would make sense.

At the foot of each bed was a metal hutch, about four feet high. It consisted of two storage shelves and a cupboard at the top with a mesh door. The hutches, like the floor, were painted gray.

"Will this be enough room for your things?" Sister Abigail asked her.

"Oh yes," said Anne-Marie. "Plenty of room. I've only got this one bag and the backpack."

She noticed there was artwork on the walls, and craft projects. Some were simple crosses made of wood and rawhide, while others were commercial posters with Christian themes. "Are we allowed to decorate the walls?"

"Yes, just as long as you keep your own things in the area above your bed."

"Where are the other girls, Sister Abigail?"

"Some of them are in Bible study, and some of them are in a crafts class we started last month. You'll get to meet them before long. You'll be thoroughly welcome here, Anne-Marie; they'll all treat you like a sister."

It seemed too good to be true. "I don't know how to thank you."

The counselor laughed. "Don't worry about that now. Why don't you make yourself at home? Get your things put away and give yourself some time to clean up."

"I'd like to. I haven't had a shower for two days."

Sister Abigail reached for and gently fingered the ends of Anne-Marie's long blond hair. "Such pretty hair. It looks like you just washed it."

"I haven't, though. Not for two days. It looks prettier when it's clean."

Abigail dropped her hand. "Well. You get settled and then come back down to my quarters. We'll have a cup of tea and get acquainted."

As soon as she was alone, Anne-Marie began shelving

her clothing in the hutch. There were two shelves but she only needed the top one. In the cupboard she put her makeup and bathroom articles, as well as her money. She discovered she'd forgotten several things she normally considered essential, such as her hair dryer, her conditioning rinse, and her eyeliner. Oh well, she reminded herself, things that were important at home were probably insignificant at Camp Shaddai.

She noticed all the beds were neatly made; some of them had quilts. The one closest to hers had some troll dolls resting on the pillow. Two had orange hair, two yellow, and one green. The green-haired one was largest. Troll dolls were *soo outré,* Anne-Marie had to wonder what kind of roommate this would be. Above the bed, on the wall, was a picture of John the Baptist exhorting listeners along the bank of the River Jordan. He looked especially wild and wooly. The picture itself looked crude, but it was professional work, crude-looking on purpose.

The bathroom turned out to be a group one, but it was very clean and there were curtains for privacy on each shower stall. A large linen closet with hinged doors was home for numerous soaps, shampoos, hair dryers, makeup kits, and tampons. Anne-Marie stared at a box of tampons; it seemed so weird not to need them anymore.

Since this cabinet was the home for hygiene items, she went to retrieve her own. She stacked them as neatly as possible in an unoccupied corner of one of the top shelves.

Anne-Marie took an extra-long shower, soaping herself slowly. When she lathered her large, well-formed breasts, she remembered with remorse how Richard relished them. But even worse, she remembered how she had always relished their power to arouse him. She soaped thoroughly in the nether regions of her loins, that treacherous location even Brother Jackson had been unable to resist.

It was disheartening to think about the craving of the flesh she not only inspired in males, but took pleasure in provoking. The person she was, had been, and might be again if her faith was weak.

After many soapings and gobs of lather, she let the hot water tumble down her torso and limbs. It felt so purifying and cleansing, as if she were washing away not just the dirt itself, but the self she was leaving behind. It felt like being born anew.

She had to borrow a towel from the closet (one more thing she hadn't thought to bring along). Sitting next to the towel were two pairs of silver scissors, one the long slim variety designed for cutting hair. Also close at hand was a box of Clairol hair coloring, currant hue. None of these things belonged to Anne-Marie, and she hadn't yet met the person to whom they did belong, but the urge to make herself over was keen. She had some money. If she did use the Clairol, she could easily replace it.

She stood in the steam from the shower stall that clouded most of the mirror. Using the towel, she wiped sections of the mist from the mirror so she could see. Her long blond hair was cheerleader hair, the legacy of Anne-Marie the worldly who strove for the look of a *Maxim* cover girl.

Firmly and surely, she cut away the lower six inches of the wet locks. Her goal was to achieve a form of blunt cut, although she knew there would be uneven edges. It didn't matter. What difference could uneven edges make here?

Enough of the mirror was clear by now to permit a full view of her body. The cross attached to the ring which pierced her navel—would Sister Abigail approve? Could the pagan part of it contaminate the Christian part? Surely not. The cross was a gift from Brother Jackson, after all, and he himself had attached it to the circle.

She returned to the shower long enough to wash her hair a second time and apply the hair color. It took ten minutes or so to set before she could wash it out. She used the time to clean the wet locks from the floor in front of the wash basins. There were paper towels for wiping down the surface.

The net result was about what she expected: a short blunt cut, more or less currant in color, with uneven edges. She liked it. "This is the new me," she said softly to the young woman in the mirror. It occurred to her as an afterthought that a new appearance would also make her more difficult to track. It was a needless thought, though, because Camp Shaddai was such a remote, sequestered place.

When Anne-Marie presented herself in Sister Abigail's quarters, the counselor did a double take. "Goodness. Look at you."

Anne-Marie felt self-conscious, but asked, "Do you like it?"

"I think it's lovely. It makes a whole new you."

"I was hoping so. That was the idea. But I never cut my own hair before, so it's pretty uneven around the edges."

"Not to worry," said Sister Abigail. "One of your dorm mates is a girl named Crystal. You'll be meeting her soon. She's very good at cutting hair, and I have an idea she'll be happy to clean up the edges. Why don't you have a seat here at the table, Anne-Marie, and I'll brew us some tea."

Anne-Marie didn't like tea, but the serenity of the environment put that concern aside. "Thank you very much," she said.

Abigail went to the far end of the long room where there was a modest kitchenette. She put the pot on the stove and got some tea bags from a cupboard. Anne-Marie could see that her beauty was even more stunning than she'd noticed before. Not only were her limbs golden tan, but they were perfectly formed with muscular definition. Not the large pumped muscles of those gross bodybuilders who strutted their stuff on ESPN and looked like male wannabes, but defined with grace and beauty. It was as if her physical radiance was God's stamp of approval, signifying her inner state of grace.

The apartment itself was a shiny one—knotty pine paneling with a high gloss and a sleeping loft above in the A-frame cavity. Besides the kitchenette, there was a dining area with a maple table and four chairs. There was a large cross made of stained wood on one wall, and a poster that said, *Whither thou goest, I will go. Thy people shall be my people, and thy God shall be my God.* Anne-Marie recognized the passage from the book of Ruth; the recognition gave her a sense of pride. The term paper on Canada geese never got finished, but her Bible knowledge was much stronger.

Sister Abigail returned with two cups of tea and a small plate of butter cookies. Anne-Marie sipped in tiny amounts.

"After the Bible study," said Sister Abigail, "the girls will come back and do a few chores in the dorm. I'm afraid you'll be assigned a few housekeeping duties of your own."

"I don't mind," Anne-Marie said immediately. "I wouldn't want to stay here without pitching in somehow."

"I didn't think you would. After that, we go to lunch in the dining hall. I think you'll like our food."

"But Sister Abigail, how am I going to pay my way? A person can't just stay here for free, can they?"

The counselor smiled before she said, "Let's not worry about that right now. It's too soon."

But Anne-Marie was accustomed to having means and was used to paying for things. "We have money. We're for sure not poor and I've got some money with me."

"The River of Life Fellowship provides the funding for our operation here," explained Abigail. "People from all over the country, even all over the world, send what money they can afford. Ten-dollar checks, on up to as much as a hundred."

Anne-Marie knew that the River of Life Fellowship had a cable television network as well as one on radio. "Does the Fellowship pay expenses for Brother Jackson?"

"Not only Brother Jackson," came the reply, "but many other evangelists as well. One of the Lord's miracles comes in the form of the generosity of small and humble people giving what they can. You leave the funding concerns up to me for now. When the time comes, if we need to talk about it, I'll be sure to let you know."

It was so comforting it almost seemed too good to be true. "Thank you," was all Anne-Marie could think to say.

Sister Abigail said, "Since you have a new 'do and a new look, why don't we think about finding a name for you to take while you're with us?"

"A new name?"

"Most of our fellowshippers like to choose a name they associate with a favorite Bible character or passage of Scripture. They do it to signify their new life in Christ; their new identity in the Lord's family. In fact, it was when I first came here twelve years ago that I chose the name Abigail."

"Abigail is a name you picked?"

"It is indeed. I wanted to find a name that would signify submission, so I thought, what could be better than the Biblical woman who gave up all to follow her Lord and Master?"

Anne-Marie wished her Biblical knowledge extended further. She knew she still had much to learn. She wasn't sure who Abigail was, in the Bible. But the idea of choosing a new name for herself, to signify her new life in Christ, excited her. "I hadn't thought of it, but I can see how it's a good idea," she said.

"One of your dorm mates, Rachel, came to us with a different name. You'll get to know her and love her. She's blessed with the gift of prophecy."

"I don't know what name I would choose," Anne-Marie admitted.

"Is Anne-Marie your real name, or is it simply Anne?"

"It's Anne. My family always left in my middle name because it was the name of my aunt on my father's side. She died young."

"I'm sorry for that. Maybe we could do something with Anne, hmm?" Sister Abigail straightened the hair above her left ear, but Anne-Marie couldn't see where anything was out of place.

Anne-Marie felt pressure, as if she ought to be able to pick an appropriate name from the Bible immediately. Otherwise, Abigail might think she was ignorant of Scripture. She glanced at the poster on the wall, before she said quietly, "Whither thou goest, I will go."

Abigail smiled broadly before she completed the passage without turning in her chair. "Thy people shall be my people, and thy God shall be my God."

"It could be Ruth," said Anne-Marie quickly. "Or maybe even Ruth Anne."

"Ruth Anne would be lovely," said Sister Abigail. "There is no more perfect example of submission to the Lord's will."

"Ruth Anne," murmured Anne-Marie quietly, while trying to down another sip of the bitter tea. She wished it had some milk or sugar in it, at least. "It symbolizes the new me.

I will be putting away my old self to be born again in the body of Christ."

"Exactly. And the body of Christ is right here, among your sisters at Shaddai."

"It's kind of like a monastery or a nunnery, huh?"

Sister Abigail replaced her broad smile with an indulgent one. "In a manner of speaking, you might say so. Humility compels us not to criticize the religious practices of others, but we think the doctrines that come from the Pope in Rome are somewhat misguided."

"I know. They believe you have to go through a priest to approach the Father."

"That's one thing. But let's not talk about it, or we might find ourselves getting negative."

Negative, Anne-Marie didn't want. But her thoughts raced, much as they did when she tried to concentrate on term papers or on reading. Secure and optimistic as this setting seemed, she couldn't completely ignore the disturbing element of her situation. Her born-again new look was also in part a disguise. Unlikely as it was that she could be traced into this sector of southern Illinois wilderness, she was a runaway. She was even an underage runaway. There would be TV reports, police, radio bulletins, milk cartons, and all the rest. The police would be looking for Brother Jackson, and her parents would be worried big-time.

She asked Sister Abigail in a quiet voice, "Have you called my parents? I have to know."

"Called your parents about what?"

Anne-Marie wondered how much she knew. How much information had Brother Jackson given her? "I just mean, people don't know I'm here. I don't want to be *turned in,* if you know what I mean. I haven't done anything wrong or broken any laws, I can promise you."

"You can promise and I can trust you," said Sister Abigail simply. "I think you're getting ahead of yourself again."

"What d'you mean?"

"Well, first you asked about costs and funding. Now you're asking me about who knows what and who ought to know what. If you need the Lord's help to find the solution to a problem you may be having, then that's what we need to be praying about."

"When I'm secure in the Lord, I'll know His will."

"Exactly. You'll know His will. That means you'll know what choices you need to make. In the meantime, Ruth Anne, remember your namesake."

"Whither thou goest," said Anne-Marie with relief, "I will go."

"Your people shall be my people, and your God, my God," added the counselor. "And now maybe it's time we lightened up a bit. Let me show you around some of the other facilities. When the girls come back, I'll introduce you."

"Good. Thank you, Sister Abigail. God bless you."

"And God bless you, Sister Ruth Anne."

June 16

In the dorm, she slept restlessly the first few nights. It was quiet but for the steady hum of window fans, which made it cool enough that she needed to pull up the thin blanket as well as the sheet. She was awake, then asleep, with frequent dreaming.

She fretted about the anxiety her parents must be feeling, even though she was certain Eleanor had called them. A part of her soul—a dark part—relished whatever discomfort they might be enduring, as if they were getting what they deserved for putting her on a contract like a criminal. She was ashamed of the feelings, though; she was certain the Lord would want her to make room in her heart to forgive them.

Since she had to urinate once or twice each night, she had to learn to navigate her way carefully between the beds, in the dark. The concrete was always cool on the soles of her feet.

In the mornings she sometimes felt low levels of nausea

that continued to inhibit her appetite. Once or twice, Sister Abigail asked her if she was disappointed with the food in the cafeteria, but she said no, the food was good. And in truth, it was. "It must be nerves," she said to the counselor.

"Everything is new, Ruth Anne," said Abigail. "You can't be expected to feel right at home immediately. Give it a little time. You'll be eating like a horse and sleeping like a baby."

Anne-Marie hoped and assumed she was right, but the assurance couldn't completely calm her raw nerves.

There was a small tabernacle down near the edge of the lake, situated in a grove of cottonwood trees. In the evenings, Sister Abigail fellowshipped with the whole group.

When Abigail preached, she wore a white muslin tunic. It reached below her hips and had long, loose sleeves, so it resembled a plain kind of choir robe. There were three crosses embroidered across the chest, the largest one flanked by smaller ones. Two floodlights attached to the sides of the stage put her in a spotlight. She seemed to shine with special radiance.

One of the first sermons Anne-Marie heard her give was a warning. Sister Abigail cautioned them that the world, and most people in it, would try to undermine their faith. "If you want respect," she said, "it won't be easy to find. Contempt *will* be easy to find, so you will need the strength to endure it and overcome it."

Anne-Marie understood how true it was. She thought of the skepticism of her parents, the smart-ass comments

Richard had delivered. Even Brooke had mocked her when Anne-Marie revealed she wanted to turn her life over to the Lord.

"Respect will have to come from within," the counselor continued. "I'm sure you know by now how hard it is to stand up for your own beliefs when the world is scornful. Praise God, though, that standing firm is not something you have to do alone. The Lord will never leave your side. He is always standing there with you, holding your hand."

As hard as Anne-Marie tried to concentrate, and as much as she could relate to the words, she found her mind wandering. She thought of her parents and Eleanor. She hoped Richard got the car back on time, with no dents or scrapes. She hoped he remembered not to leave any cigarette butts in the ashtray. She even thought of clothing and makeup she wished she'd remembered to bring along. She shook her head; in school, she was always this way. She knew the Lord wanted her undivided attention.

"Because the Lord gives all," Sister Abigail was saying, "He expects all. He didn't die on the cross just so people could go to church on Sunday morning or put a few dollars in the Salvation Army kettle at Christmas. The Lord of your life means the center of your life, not just a hobby or part-time activity. If your goal is to follow Him, you will have infinite joy, but you may not have much comfort."

It was that same night, at the conclusion of fellowship, when they joined hands in a circle for closing prayer, that

Rachel began to speak in tongues. She was a gaunt and mystical creature who slept in the bed closest to Anne-Marie's.

When Rachel spoke in tongues it was a disturbing combination of clicking and humming. There weren't any discernible words, but there was an obvious connection to an unspeakably mystical force: *clickety-click-click* while maintaining a deep-throated hum almost like a background of studio musicians. It stirred Anne-Marie to the depths to realize that whatever discomfort she might be feeling in this period of transition, she was truly in a place of spiritual power so great it brought forth the Mysteries of the Lord Himself.

After fellowship there was at least an hour before lights out. It turned out the Clairol she had "borrowed" without asking permission belonged to Crystal, the girl who liked to cut hair. Crystal was very fat and wore geeky glasses. Her thighs rippled with cellulite. "I'm sorry I took it without asking," Anne-Marie told her.

"Don't worry, I wasn't going to use it anyway. At least not on myself. Sister Abigail said you might like me to trim your hair."

"Would you? I like it this short and this color, but I cut it myself. I guess that's pretty obvious, huh?"

Crystal cocked her head so she could examine Anne-Marie's hair a little more carefully. She pushed her stubborn glasses back up the bridge of her nose. "I've seen worse," she said. "Come on, let's go back to the dorm and even up those ends."

"That would be great."

Crystal gave Anne-Marie a hand mirror to hold while she did the trimming. She was deft and confident while she worked. "Have you been here before?" Anne-Marie asked her.

"This is my fourth summer. One year I was here all summer, but this year I'll only be here for six weeks. My parents are taking me to Barbados in the middle of July."

"Do your parents like you to come here?"

"My parents love for me to come here. I have problems at school sometimes. People make fun of me and tease me. I always try to laugh it off, but it's hard when people are always teasing you and being cruel."

Anne-Marie could imagine why. With that bulk and those ornery glasses, which kept slipping down her nose, she would be an easy target for high school classmates. "I'm sorry," said Anne-Marie softly, and for more reasons than one. She could remember when she herself, not so long ago, was one of those who teased the geeks and played practical jokes, sometimes even cruel ones. She thought of the conversation she'd had with Sara Curtis when she tried to apologize for that kind of behavior.

"Sorry for what?" Crystal asked.

"Just sorry that . . . that people treat you that way." She moved quickly to change the subject: "I have problems in school, too."

"You do?" Crystal sounded doubtful.

"Maybe not the same kind as you. I have trouble with my grades. I get low grades." She stopped short of revealing that she'd failed to graduate.

"But you're so beautiful, Anne-Marie. You must be like real popular."

"Why do you think that?"

"I can just tell. I have a radar about these things. Girls as beautiful as you are always very popular in school."

Anne-Marie could feel herself blushing. She wondered if the red creeping up the back of her neck was visible to her new friend with the scissors. "Beautiful has to be what you are on the inside," she finally said. "It's like Sister Abigail said. Besides, whatever my looks are, I've always gotten low grades in school. The way the teachers and counselors put it, I'm an academic underachiever."

"You have low self-esteem too, then," declared Crystal. Anne-Marie felt certain the pleasure in her voice was unintentional. "I didn't think it ever happened to the popular girls."

"If I told you about my older sister, you'd understand why."

Crystal was at work on Anne-Marie's bangs. "Hold real still now," she cautioned. "Whenever we're here at Camp Shaddai, I'm always reminded it's only how I look in God's eyes that really counts. If I'm fat, what difference does it make? If He is for me, who can be against me?"

"It's true, huh," said Anne-Marie, knowing her own parents would never be able to find any enthusiasm for Camp Shaddai. They would probably think it was just a cult site, out of balance.

Anne-Marie was given latrine duty the first week. It was her job to clean the toilets, the sinks, the shower stalls, the mirrors, and the vanity surfaces. Ironically, it was something she knew how to do. When she'd been a cheerleader, Mrs. Stiles, the sponsor, used to make them clean the bathrooms of the girls' locker room whenever she caught them smoking.

Anne-Marie was amazed at the difference. What had been a disgusting form of punishment back at her school was suddenly a joy in service to the Lord. No job was too humble or disgusting if it was conducted in His service. Hadn't Brother Jackson said exactly that about fixing tractors and mowing grass?

She laughed once or twice when this fundamental distinction actually filled her with a sense of honor. It even kept her close to the toilets, convenient for those rare occasions when she felt the nausea.

Once when she was cleaning sinks and mirrors, she watched Rachel showering. Rachel didn't bother pulling the curtain closed. She seemed utterly unself-conscious, even though her wiry body was extremely boyish. She didn't even shave her armpits.

Anne-Marie tried not to stare, but the mirror gave her such an easy view, she couldn't help herself. On Rachels' left shoulder blade was a finely drawn blue tattoo, approximately six inches long, of Christ on the cross. Drops of blood fell from his side in red ink. The small words in clear letters below the tattoo declared, *This blood's for you.*

Anne-Marie longed to know her better because of her gift of prophecy and her knowledge of the Mysteries. The tattoo seemed to be an opening for conversation. "Where did you get the tattoo?" she asked.

"In a Christian tattoo parlor in St. Louis," replied Rachel.

"They've got tattoo parlors just for Christians?"

"It's the only one I've seen." Rachel was toweling off, rubbing her straight, unkempt hair. Except that it was black, its disheveled condition might have belonged to one of the troll dolls that rested on her bed. "They have the head of Christ, the cross itself, even the sacraments of the Last Supper. About any religious image you can think of."

Anne-Marie had pierced ears and the pierced navel which held her hoop and cross, but she'd never gotten a tattoo. She'd decided long ago that if she ever got one, she'd want it on her ankle, not her shoulder blade.

June 17

Just before dawn, when her restlessness seemed most acute, Anne-Marie dreamed of Brother Jackson. She dreamed of his tractor, and the oil rig, and the spiritual ecstasy of their physical union in his small bed. Half awake again, but still asleep, she was in the trancelike condition of the twilight zone: She longed not so much for the memory itself as for the cosmic, haloed effect which the dream brought with it.

Rachel had given Anne-Marie one of the troll dolls with wild, yellow hair. When she had trouble sleeping, Anne-Marie would roll onto her side and squeeze the doll tightly between her palms like a tension reliever.

Eventually, she was wide awake in spite of her efforts otherwise. Anne-Marie turned on her side to discover Rachel looking at her. "You were talking in your sleep," Rachel informed her.

"What was I saying?"

"You kept saying *brother.* Sometimes you said *father.*"

"Brother? Father?" This was embarrassing. Anne-Marie swung herself into the seated position on the edge of her bed. "What else did I say?"

"Nothing, I don't think." Of all the sisters in her group, Rachel was the most mysterious. She seemed to live almost exclusively on an ethereal level. At times when she spoke to Anne-Marie, it was almost as if she was looking straight through her and beyond, into another dimension. Sister Abigail had said Rachel was graced with the gift of prophecy, and Anne-Marie had no problem believing it.

Anne-Marie could feel how the troll doll was mashed nearly flat; she kept it under the sheet so Rachel wouldn't see its battered condition. In truth, with her wild hair and wild eyes, Rachel bore a striking resemblance to her dolls.

"Do you have dreams?" Anne-Marie asked her.

"I have dreams and I have visions. Sometimes the dreams and the visions become one."

"You have the gift of prophecy, don't you?"

"I have the gift of prophecy," Rachel confirmed matter-of-factly. She paused long enough to take a tissue and blow her nose. "Sometimes, though, the gift is like a curse."

"How is it like a curse?"

"Because I can't control it. Visions come to me. They may come directly from the Lord Himself, but they come on their own. Sometimes they are very troubling and I feel responsible."

"You mean like a psychic who might see a crime being committed but can't do anything in time to stop it?"

"Something like that." Rachel was on her side again, pushing some of the unruly bangs from her eyes. "I dream the incubus."

"What does that mean?" asked Anne-Marie.

"The incubus is a demon who troubles young women in their sleep. He is capable of seducing them with the demon seed."

Anne-Marie felt scared. She had goose flesh. "What does that mean? What does the incubus look like?"

"He can change his form. That's Satan's power. Sometimes he is ugly and disgusting with great wings like bat wings. He wants seduction by terror. But sometimes he appears in the form of a man who's handsome. That's his power."

"But what does he do?"

"He can seduce. He can trouble young girls and women in their sleep and bring the demon seed."

Anne-Marie didn't wait to hear any more. She had to go to the bathroom, and right away. Rachel's level of contact with the Mysteries was too troubling. After she used the toilet she stepped into the shower. *The incubus?* It was too disturbing, and especially so right after her sublime dream of her union with Brother Jackson.

Anne-Marie made a headband in arts and crafts. Since she'd always been good at art, the headband was a work of special quality. She used a scarlet ribbon, two inches wide, which for some unknown reason had ended up at the bottom of her tote bag. The ribbon was actually a belt for a red dress that was hanging at home in her closet.

The headband she crafted wrapped around her head horizontally above her ears, like an American Indian headband or a hippy one from the sixties. Using white paint and a very fine detail brush, she painted the words *El Shaddai* carefully in block letters. She applied the words in two places, so when she tied on the headband, they were bold on both sides of her head. The extra ribbon was left to trail down the back of her neck.

Not only did she love the headband and the way it looked around her new hairdo, it gave her the opportunity to speak for the first time in share group, where the sisters were urged to confess sins and join the group in prayers for forgiveness. Sometimes the sins were minor and current, while others might be long-concealed and only revealed with great courage and trust.

Anne-Marie told her group what the headband represented. "The ribbon comes from a red dress I used to wear to parties and out on dates. It symbolizes the old me, the worldly me, the person who loved to party and was always willful. I think red is the right color for that symbolism. The white symbolizes the Lord, who is now in control of my life. White means purity. The purity of my new life in the Lord is meant to be on top of the old red. The new me replaces the old."

All the members of her group were thoroughly

impressed, particularly Crystal, who was as skilled at art as she was at haircutting. "It's not only the meaning of the headband," she declared, "but also how artistic it is."

"I've always been good at art," Anne-Marie admitted. "It's the other subjects that I always have trouble with."

Sister Abigail told them she wanted them to choose a "prayer target" for the day. "It doesn't matter who you pick," she said. "Just choose someone you know who needs prayer. Or, if you'd rather, it could be someone you don't know but might have read about or seen on the news. A victim of a natural disaster, or a political leader who needs the Lord's guidance to make ethical decisions."

"When do we pray for them?" asked Crystal.

"Anytime during the day," answered the counselor, with a smile. "Whenever you have free time, whenever you're working on a chore. Maybe when you're studying your Bible on your own. Keep this person in your prayers throughout the day. The Lord rejoices when we pray for others as well as for ourselves."

Anne-Marie was uncertain about the assignment, but Rachel spoke right up. "I will be praying for my brother."

Sister Abigail said, "Rachel, wouldn't you like to pick someone else for a change?"

"I can't help it," replied Rachel. "If he's in prison, his only salvation is if he gives his life over to the Lord. 'I was in prison and you came to me.' This is my only way to go to him."

Around the circle, one by one, the sisters named the

person who would be their prayer target for the day. Anne-Marie didn't hear most of them; she was racking her brain for an appropriate choice.

Finally, when Sister Abigail turned to her, Anne-Marie said, "I'd like to pray for Chris Weems."

"Is this a friend of yours from home?"

"Not really a friend, but I know him. When I go back, I hope to know him better. He's gay, but he wishes he wasn't."

"The Lord will bless you for this," said Abigail. "If God can hate the sin while still loving the sinner, so can we."

Private meditation always followed share group. Anne-Marie took her Bible and found her way to a private place she liked, a footbridge in the woods. It was a rustic, rickety bridge, about thirty feet long, which spanned a creek bed. Since there hadn't been much rain lately, the bed was now a dry wash. But there was a deep shade from the mature cottonwood trees along the bank.

Anne-Marie opened her Bible just as soon as she took a seat on the edge of the bridge and let her feet dangle over the side. The bookmark which Sister Abigail had given her bore the words of an old-time preacher: *Preach faith until you have faith.* The words intrigued her. If you had doubts, the thing to do was to act as if you didn't. If you declared your faith when the doubts occurred, it would only guarantee the permanent faith which came from submission.

She pondered the message on the bookmark so repeatedly that she was looking at Scripture passages without actually reading them. She finally remembered her promise to pray for Chris Weems.

The words didn't come easily, even though she tried her best to get focused. She couldn't decide if she should pray for his peace of mind, his power to change out of the gay lifestyle, the Lord to forgive him, or simply to *pray* for him. "Lord, I just want to lift up Chris Weems," she said aloud. After that no new words seemed to come, so she repeated the same ones.

She wondered if she should pray for Richard instead. She knew him better, knew some of his self-destructive habits, and knew the way he more or less flipped life off. But she had promised to pray for Chris, so she kept trying.

After lunch, she talked to Sister Abigail in her quarters. It was always a privilege when she counseled you all alone. Sister was polite enough to offer tea again, so Anne-Marie was polite enough to sip it from time to time.

Anne-Marie began by telling her she'd had a dream of Brother Jackson and how she'd tried to preserve it by not waking up. It felt so easy to tell her about private things. "Do you believe the Lord visits us in dreams, Sister Abigail?"

"Of course he does, Ruth Anne. But you said it wasn't really a dream, but a recollection of actual events."

"It was a real experience, that's true. But it was the feeling about it which seemed so special. When it was dream-like, it felt almost like it was holy." Then she revealed the dream to Abigail.

Sister Abigail returned the teapot to the counter by the

stove before she responded. “Ruth Anne, you’re describing fornication. It would be a stretch to call that holy, wouldn’t it?”

Fornication sounded like such a dirty word. “I know, but it was different somehow. What happened between Brother Jackson and me was on a high plane, like it was meant to be.”

Sister Abigail smiled. “Sometimes we call that lust, dear. It has something to do with being aroused. Do you recall what the Scripture tells us about wolves in sheep’s clothing?”

“Of course I do, but we could never call Brother Jackson a wolf.”

“Of course we couldn’t. I would never suggest we could.”

It wasn’t lust any more than it was fornication, though. She began to regret bringing the subject up, because it was so hard to express her feelings. “I just wish I could communicate better, Sister Abigail. I know how vague it must seem.” Anne-Marie took a tiny sip of the tea, just to moisten her dry lips.

Sister Abigail was nibbling on a butter cookie. Before she spoke again, she used the tip of her little finger to remove a crumb at the corner of her mouth. “Ruth Anne, are you sure the events you just described to me actually happened?”

“Am I sure?”

“That’s what I’m asking. Are you absolutely certain?”

Anne-Marie hesitated. “Sister Abigail,” she finally said, summoning the courage, “I’m pregnant. I’m going to have his baby.”

Abigail sat up straight in her chair. Before she answered at all, she went to the counter again to carve another lemon slice. At the table, she squeezed its contents into her teacup. "Who knows about this?" she asked.

"Nobody. You're the first person I've told."

"I want you to think carefully. You haven't told any friends or family members?"

"Not about the Brother Jackson part," Anne-Marie replied quickly.

Sister Abigail asked, "Which part, then?" Her smile looked forced.

"I haven't told anyone else that Brother Jackson is the father. I told my sister and a counselor that I'm pregnant. I also told a former boyfriend, but that was just because I needed a ride."

With her elbows planted on her knees, Abigail searched Anne-Marie's eyes. "Ruth Anne, you're accusing Brother Jackson of seducing you. Let me ask you one more time if you're certain."

"But I'm not accusing, I'm only sharing with you. I'm sharing something that seemed beautiful between us like it came from a higher power. Why do you keep asking me if I'm certain?"

"Because you began by calling it a dream. Can you be sure that's not what it was?"

Anne-Marie wondered why most of her serious conversations felt like she was seated on the witness stand. "It was a dreamlike memory of something that actually happened. Hasn't that ever happened to you?"

Abigail was still wearing the patient smile. "You were in that in-between state which is half awake but half asleep. Sometimes, in that condition, our dreams get confused with our realities."

"I feel certain about it," said Anne-Marie. "But I do know what you're saying," she had to admit.

"Sometimes we dream about things we long for, which makes them seem as real as events which actually occur. May I ask you a personal question?"

Anne-Marie looked up. "Sure, why not?"

"Have you been intimate with boys? Young men? Have you been a sexually active person?"

She looked down again, ashamed; her answer was slow in coming. "A few times, yes I have."

"And did it give you pleasure?"

"I don't understand."

"I'm asking you if you enjoy sexual intercourse."

There wasn't any point in lying. "Yes," she said. Squirming, she found herself recalling memories of Richard. He wasn't the only one, but he was the most recent. And when it came to having sex, she would be lying if she tried to claim she merely put up with it. Oh no. She enjoyed Richard's body and the pleasure it brought to the point that she had often been the romantic aggressor.

Once again, she remembered smoking pot by the lake

and then having sex. Not to mention the times when they skipped out of school together for trysts in the woods, and she ended up getting suspended for truancy. School suspensions were not the issue here, but Anne-Marie's confusion had reached the point where she wasn't sure what the issue was.

She thought to add immediately, "But that was the old me. That wasn't Ruth Anne."

Sister Abigail smiled a little broader before she said, "That was before you put on the whole armor of God?"

Anne-Marie smiled, too. "That's what I'm saying." She ran her fingers through her hair, only to be reminded how short it was now.

Abigail said, "Maybe some part of you longed for Brother Jackson physically because you respected and admired him so."

"But why would I do that?"

"Maybe you wouldn't, but the Evil One would."

"You mean Satan."

"Precisely. He is reluctant to let go of you. He doesn't want you born again. He understands that sexual pleasure is part of your past, so he tries to seduce the old you."

Her earlier conversation with Rachel suddenly popped into her head, the one about an incubus. Seduction and demons during the night, troubling all your dreams. She said, "You're saying Satan would try to use my own past against me."

"Of course, just as surely as a hunter would set a snare to catch a rabbit. If there's a corner of you that is physically attracted to Brother Jackson, why would Satan pass up the opportunity to use it? The strategy is too easy."

Anne-Marie could see the logic of this counsel, but it only confused her more. *Could it be?* she asked herself. *Was such a thing possible?* "Maybe it really *was* a dream," she speculated out loud. "You're saying Satan could use my own subconscious mind to lead me to destruction."

Abigail leaned back in her chair before resting her cup on her knee. She picked at a piece of thread on her blue cotton shorts. "He's not called the Prince of Darkness for nothing, is he?"

Anne-Marie thought again about Brother Jackson and the silver cross. What about that cross? But even the bliss seemed to be fading. "I'll have to pray about it," she finally said.

"We'll all have to pray about it. Individually, as well as together. If Satan wants another foothold in you, we intend to make it very tough on him." Now Abigail was laughing gaily.

Anne-Marie thanked her. Her confusion was on hold. Sister Abigail squeezed her hand before kissing her cheek. "Don't forget," she whispered. "The Spirit is stronger than any demon."

June 20

Immediately after lunch there was a traumatic scene in the parking lot. Out near the rustic arch on the blacktop, where Brother Jackson had delivered Anne-Marie some days ago, there seemed to be a confrontation between Sister Abigail and the parents of a member of their group named Michelle.

Anne-Marie watched the animated conversation from beneath the shade of a generous oak tree, while sitting on a wooden bench next to Jessica. The two girls were too far away to hear what was being said, but the body language was dramatic enough.

The man, a well-dressed handsome figure, was stowing Michelle's gear in the trunk of the car, a charcoal-colored Continental. Michelle had taken a place in the backseat, but she was in tears, sobbing with her face in her hands. The spectacle triggered a long-forgotten memory: Anne-Marie remembered when she was young, maybe ten or eleven, and she'd gotten homesick at church camp. Her parents came to get her after she'd called home about three times. As soon as they'd told her she didn't have to stay any longer, she'd cried tears of relief. This was different; Michelle's tears were not those of relief, but despair.

"What's going on?" Anne-Marie asked Jessica.

Jessica was a veteran of several summers at Camp Shaddai. "Her parents are taking her home against her will. It happens sometimes."

"Why does it happen?"

"Some people think that what we do here is part of a cult activity. Maybe I should say *most* people. They believe Camp Shaddai is a cult."

"But that's stupid. Why would they think that? Why would it be a cult if your goal is to have the Lord at the center of your life?"

"I know," said Jessica. "But it happens. I've seen it before."

Anne-Marie shuddered. She could just imagine how quickly her own parents would swoop down on Shaddai and carry her away against her will. This thought made her more uncomfortable when she realized she still hadn't called Eleanor like she'd promised she would. "What can we do for Michelle?" she asked Jessica. "It's so sad when people just can't understand."

"Can't, or won't," Jessica replied. "We can pray for her. I'm sure tonight at fellowship meeting, we will lift her up in prayer above all other concerns."

It was still sad. Anne-Marie watched the two parents

gesturing in animated fashion at Sister Abigail, who only stood humbly with her hands joined behind her back. Anne-Marie couldn't imagine Sister Abigail's humiliation at this moment, yet she still seemed so poised. Anne-Marie's admiration was total. *Praise Him in all things,* the Bible said. It was the only appropriate passage she could think of for the moment.

Later that afternoon, when crafts were over, Rachel took Anne-Marie on an expedition. "I'll show you the mountain-top," she declared.

They walked slowly down a dense and rocky incline until they found their way to the crude footbridge where Anne-Marie liked to spend her private prayer and meditation time. The bridge, made of aging boards, was framed up by rough gray two-by-fours.

They sat side by side on the edge. "I've seen this gorge full of water," said Rachel, "right after it rains. We haven't had any rain for a long time."

"I'd like to see it full of water," said Anne-Marie. "I could stand in it just like the River Jordan. You could be John the Baptist."

Rachel giggled. "I guess I've got the hair for it." She lifted herself up until she was standing erect on one of the two-by-fours that formed a railing.

"You better get down," Anne-Marie warned her.

Rachel was balancing with her arms extended, like a tightrope walker in a circus. She was giggling while she took tiny heel-and-toe steps. She might have been a drunk driver taking a "walk-the-line" test for a state trooper. "I've done this before," she told Anne-Marie. "Don't worry."

"But I am worried. Come on, please get down."

"I've had dreams about this bridge," said Rachel.

"What dreams?"

"Vision dreams. Dreams of the Spirit." Still walking very slowly, heel-and-toe, with horizontal arms for balance.

"What visions?" Anne-Marie asked urgently. "What dreams of the Spirit?"

"I dream the pale horse sometimes. He is running across this bridge with loud, pounding hooves. He is running and running, and getting all lathered with that white foam horses get around the neck."

And behold, a pale horse, Anne-Marie recalled from the Book of Revelation, one of Abigail's favorite Scripture sources. *And its rider's name was Death, and Hades followed after.* She looked up at Rachel, who was now trying her balancing act with her eyes closed.

All of a sudden, Anne-Marie was very frightened. It wasn't just about the disturbing dream, either. Wearing just her worn overalls, and her hair so wild, Rachel looked like a supernatural figure who might have been an out-of-time female version of John the Baptist. She looked for all the world like a creature who could disappear into these southern Illinois woodlands and feed on locusts and tree bark or whatever it was that had sustained the ancient Biblical prophet.

"Rachel, please get down from there. You're scaring me."

"Okay." And down she jumped. She seemed so light on her feet, but then Anne-Marie guessed she couldn't weigh much more than ninety pounds anyway.

Once they crossed the bridge, and another smaller one later, which crossed another shallow dry wash, Rachel told her to follow her to the mountaintop. It was a long and rocky climb, cut into the side of an enormous limestone deposit that formed a crease along the mountain. Anne-Marie was reminded again of the Ozarks, from past family vacations.

At times the footing was well defined and firm, but at other times they had to bend over so as to squeeze themselves around and between large rocks and boulders. Nevertheless, Anne-Marie could see far enough ahead to know where they were going.

The climb lasted at least twenty minutes, but when they reached the top it was worth the effort. It was truly a breathtaking vista. The entire lake was visible from here, and it was huge. From this vantage point, Anne-Marie realized that Camp Shaddai occupied only a small niche of the timber at the southern shore.

They were standing on a plateau of rock that was amazingly level but not much larger than their front porch back at home. Maybe fifteen by thirty feet. Anne-Marie could see that the drop-off was sheer, a sheet of vertical limestone with the lake at least 150 feet below.

“Don’t get too close to the edge,” Rachel advised.

“Don’t worry,” said Anne-Marie with a nervous laugh. “I’ll be staying right here next to you.”

“Sister Abigail doesn’t like us to come here.”

“She doesn’t?”

“Not without supervision. She doesn’t think it’s safe.”

“I won’t tell if you don’t.”

“My lips are sealed,” said Rachel with a laugh. “Now look up. Look the other way.”

Anne-Marie looked up. Another sheet of cliffs, just as vertical and just as sheer, rose above them so high it nearly seemed to pierce the sky. Stunning as it was, it gave her vertigo, so she had to look away.

“I come here sometimes by myself,” said Rachel. “The Lord is here. He’s always here, just as surely as you are right now.”

Anne-Marie was looking at her new friend. Rachel had a nice complexion and nice teeth. If she took more interest in her appearance, she could be attractive. But that was a trivial notion; Rachel was connected intimately to the Spirit, which meant she could confidently put aside the things of the world. What value could trifling things like makeup or jewelry have if you were living in a state of God’s grace?

“I see why you call it the mountaintop,” said Anne-Marie. “It’s like the God of Abraham on his very own mountain peak.”

"It is," confirmed Rachel. "God of his very God on the peak of his very mountain. It is the El of Abraham's mountain, the one God ever and Eternal."

"It's El Shaddai," murmured Anne-Marie reverently. And saying so, she thought achingly of that afternoon in Brother Jackson's quarters where he had the poster of El Shaddai, the mountain penetrating the clouds and the clouds forming rings like haloes. It had been the defining moment of her life, the living union of spirit and flesh, and someday she would be able to explain it so people could understand.

The two of them lay on their backs, looking up at the blue sky. Stubborn limbs of scrubby pine extended from some of the crevices along the cliff. "Is this your first year here?" Anne-Marie asked her.

"No, I was here last year. This is my second summer."

"Are you going to be here all summer?"

"Oh yeah, I wouldn't be anywhere else. I'll be here right up to Labor Day, right up to when I go back to school. I'm only a junior because I got a year behind."

"How did that happen?" Anne-Marie asked her, thinking uncomfortably of her own academic shortcomings.

"I was on the street. It got me a year behind. Then they found me a good foster home, the first real good one I ever had."

"Who are you living with now?"

"A pastor and his wife. They pastor the River of Life

Tabernacle in Clayton. That's a suburb down by St. Louis. It's the first loving home I've ever known."

"What about your parents?" Anne-Marie asked her.

"That's a long story. My dad was gone, and my mother was doing so many drugs she was in detox programs half the time. That's when I ended up in one foster home or another."

"You don't have to talk about it if you don't want to. It's probably none of my business."

"I don't mind," Rachel answered. She let out a long breath before she continued, "It's just like so complicated. I was doing drugs, too. Lots of them. My brother got me started on drugs. He was dealing. That's why he's in prison. He was convicted twice for dealing and now he's got a fourteen-year sentence."

"That's why you pray for him."

"That's why. If he can accept Jesus as his Lord and Savior, he will behave like a model prisoner. You can get early parole for good behavior."

Anne-Marie shook her head. She knew of lives ruined by drugs. It was stupid how she herself had smoked pot and even crack on occasion with Richard. It was the kind of "approval" behavior which had characterized her past. She asked Rachel, "So what happened after all the drugs and your brother going to prison?"

"I was on the street. You could even say I was homeless. There was a homeless old guy named Otis who kind of watched over me, let me sleep in his van sometimes, et cetera. But all the authorities could think was that he was taking advantage of me. It was sad."

"What did they do to him?"

"They put him in jail. After that he was in detox I think, but I never did find out for sure. Anyway, right after that, I got placed with Pastor Al and Marie. They sent me here to spend the summer last year."

"Was that when you became a Christian?"

For the first time Rachel smiled so broadly she seemed to glow. "Yeah, it was. It was one night in June after a tabernacle meeting when I was filled with the Holy Ghost and speaking in tongues. It took my breath away. It was like I was lifted onto a different plane, a totally spiritual one. My life has never been the same since."

"Was that when you knew you had the gift of prophecy?"

"No, that came a little later. I think it was about the first of August. I woke up one morning with a vision of my mom in the company of two shining angels. It was like they were suspended in the air, all three of them. I didn't know it had a meaning, it was just like real spiritual."

"So what was the meaning?"

"Two days later, I got a call from some social worker in St. Louis. My mother had died, and they were calling all the next of kin."

"I'm sorry your mother died, I really am."

"So am I, but she's with the Lord now, and her life was

hard. Real hard. What with the drugs and all the other failures in her life, praise Him she's now at peace."

"Praise Him," Anne-Marie seconded. She stretched her arms above her head. She felt at peace and mellow like she hadn't felt for weeks, convinced now of the rightness of her decision to let Brother Jackson bring her here. There were sources of spiritual support here that she could never expect to find anywhere else.

Even so, there was risk. Anne-Marie couldn't get the scene with Michelle and her parents out of her mind. She asked Rachel if she'd ever seen anything like it before.

"Sure," said her mysterious friend, with a shrug. "I've seen it. Last summer, it happened twice. Once to this girl from St. Louis and another time to a girl from Dubuque, Iowa."

"So what happened?"

"Their parents just found out where they were and came to take them. People think Camp Shaddai is like a cult or something. They can't understand."

"But why would they think it's a cult?"

"Because it's Spirit-filled. Spirit-filled living is always a threat to comfortable churchgoers."

"It's sad, huh?"

"Sure. But it's like Sister Abigail says, if you decide to pick up the cross and carry it, life is never easy."

Anne-Marie kept silent for several moments. She couldn't even imagine the shame and humiliation she would have to endure if her parents found her and took her home.

Rachel interrupted these thoughts. "What's that?" She was pointing to the cross linked to the ring in Anne-Marie's navel.

Briefly, Anne-Marie told the story of how Brother Jackson had given it to her as a gift, and secured it to the ring which was already there. After summarizing these details, she gulped and added, "There's a baby beneath it."

"There is? You're pregnant?"

"Sure am. The father is the holy evangelist who gave me the cross. It seems like a sign to me."

"It does seem like a sign. Is that why you came here?"

"He brought me here to stay for a while until he finishes a mission in Oklahoma. He'll be back in a week or two."

"And you're sort of here on retreat to pray about what you need to do next?"

"Yes. How did you know?"

"It just seems like the obvious," Rachel replied. Then she laughed. "It doesn't take a vision to figure that out."

Anne-Marie laughed, too, just before giving Rachel a squeeze on the arm. "God loves you and I love you," she said with accelerating giddiness.

"The Lord bless you, Anne-Marie, all the way home. You know what? We better be starting back or we'll be late for supper."

Supper, Anne-Marie thought. For the first time in oh so long, a meal sounded great. "Let's go then," she said. "I'm hungry."

June 23

One night at evening tabernacle, Sister Abigail preached a sermon on the danger of committee Christianity. Like Brother Jackson, she never called her talks "sermons." The preferred terminology was always "fellowshipping with her flock" or "sharing the Spirit."

"The Lord is never happy with tepid religion," she began, "any more than you would be with a tepid shower. How many of us would be happy taking a shower in chilly water?"

The light was shining on her as she sat on her high stool on the stage; the light that gave her the angelic aura also attracted the bugs and kept them away from her. "Too many people who call themselves Christians want the blessings of God's grace, but want that benefit without effort. They go to church on Sunday mornings some of the time. They serve on a committee, perhaps, as long as it doesn't interfere with their bridge club or their golf game. They put money in the collection plate, but rarely, if ever, an amount that causes them any sacrifice."

Anne-Marie thought of her parents immediately. Sister

Abigail couldn't have described them any more accurately if she'd known them all her life. She also remembered vividly the words of Brother Jackson when he described the "committee Christians" who filled up the organized theological seminaries.

"The Lord's sacrifice for us was ultimate," Sister Abigail continued. "He wants followers on fire for Him, not on low heat. He gave His life, He suffered the pain and humiliation of the cross, all so that we might love Him and serve Him and enter His Kingdom. When we choose to follow Him, we pledge to take up his cross."

Anne-Marie was sitting next to Rachel, who was beginning to speak in tongues. Just an irregular, guttural murmuring, very breathy, and not so loud as to disturb the focus of the meeting. Sister Abigail concluded her remarks by warning the girls not to be seduced by those whose brand of religion was the "armchair" kind, like sitting in a recliner and operating a television with a remote control.

Anne-Marie felt like Abigail's words were meant specifically for her. The real Christians, those who followed the Lord unconditionally, those who put Him at the center of their lives, they were the ones who could point to that fixed moment in time when they became Christians.

It was the one thing people like her parents could never understand, and probably what Sister Abigail meant was that the cross to bear was heavy when people called you "unbalanced" or members of a "cult." Or the "Christian Right."

At the close of the meeting, when it was time for prayer

circle, Anne-Marie found herself praying out loud for the first time. She began by lifting up Chris Weems, praying that someday, somehow, he would find the Spirit leading him to change out of the gay lifestyle.

Holding Rachel's hand on her right and Crystal's on her left, she felt the surge of the circle. She found the words. "Lord Jesus," she began by saying, "we just give you all the praise and glory. We thank you, Father, for the gift of the Spirit and all the other gifts which bless our lives. I'd like to lift up Michelle and her parents. I just pray you give her parents the light to understand that her new life in you is not a rejection of them. Help them understand, Lord, understand and forgive."

And then she was finished. She wasn't sure by now if her prayer was offered for Michelle and her parents or for herself. It didn't matter. She felt both of her hands get a squeeze of affirmation. Standing in the light, Sister Abigail was smiling broadly at her.

The next morning, Anne-Marie awoke early and took a long, hot shower while her dormitory mates were still sleeping. She felt how hard and tight her belly had become. It wasn't expanded; it was still flat as a board. But it was firmer. *There's a child growing there,* she reminded herself. It seemed so remarkable she repeated it out loud: "The child is growing."

It represented a different dimension of being pregnant,

this firm feeling. At least physically. She no longer had the morning nausea, and her appetite was returning daily. Physically, she felt better.

With a special energy, she lathered her loins several times over—those parts which were ever the reminder of her extraordinary sin. Again, she wanted it to be an act of purification. But it couldn't really be. It was an empty act because it was so after-the-fact. Like the people who sprayed their mouths with breath freshener after every cigarette they smoked. It couldn't really change anything, not in any lasting way.

She returned to her bed, wrapped in a large, fluffy towel. She noticed Rachel writhing in her sleep and moaning. Anne-Marie sat down on the edge of her bed and placed the tattered troll doll on her pillow. Suddenly, Rachel was awake, lying on her side and staring straight at her. She propped her head with her hand.

"Were you dreaming the incubus?" Anne-Marie asked her apprehensively. She whispered so as not to wake the others.

"Not the incubus," Rachel whispered back. "I was dreaming the pale horse on the bridge."

"What is the incubus like?" Anne-Marie asked.

"I said I wasn't dreaming it."

"I know, but I want you to tell me," Anne-Marie persisted.

Rachel blew her nose on a tissue before she responded. "He can take any form. That's the demon in him. He's not limited because he's one of Satan's minions."

"But you said he was a hideous creature with nasty wings like a bat."

"Sometimes. That's when he takes the scary form."

"Brother Jackson is the father of my baby," declared Anne-Marie suddenly, in a voice too loud.

"Shhh," Rachel reminded her. "I said I dreamed the incubus, but that doesn't mean it has to be a vision. Every dream is not a prophecy."

"How do you tell the difference?"

"Sometimes I can't. Remember, I told you the gift is not always cool. Sometimes it's more like a curse."

"And you never dreamed it about me, Rachel. Tell me that's so."

"That's so. I never dreamed the incubus and you together."

"What about the pale horse on the bridge? Doesn't that mean death?"

"Maybe, if it's a vision or a prophecy."

"You said you've had the dream several times," Anne-Marie was quick to remind her. "Does that mean there will be death? Someone will die?"

"I can't say for sure. You're real worked up this morning. Are you scared of death?"

"Oh yes, aren't you?"

"No. If you die in the arms of the Lord, He will simply take you home to eternal peace."

It was reassuring. Anne-Marie repeated Rachel's words. ". . . He will simply take you home to eternal peace."

"Exactly," said Rachel, with a smile. She took a futile

swipe at her noncompliant shock of hair. Others in the dorm were beginning to stir, so they dropped the discussion.

Crystal cut Anne-Marie's hair again. This time she fashioned a more careful, shingled effect to achieve a more chic cut. Anne-Marie didn't ask for the favor, but Crystal said she'd like to do it.

"I'm going to be a cosmetologist," she said. "When school starts in the fall, I'll only be taking two academic courses, and the rest of the time will be all vocational."

"I think you'll be good at it, Crystal. I think you have the gift."

Crystal worked her scissors and comb swiftly at the nape of Anne-Marie's neck. "When we take vocational classes, we get to be in another part of the building. It's a better place for big geeks like me to hang out. We don't get teased there as much." She was laughing.

"Why are you calling yourself a big geek?"

"Because that's what I am. But it's okay. That's one reason I love it here at Camp Shaddai. If you have the Lord inside of you, nobody cares what you look like on the outside. Did you already graduate, Anne-Marie?"

"I was supposed to, but then I needed summer school to make up some missed credits."

"Did you go through graduation ceremonies with your class?"

"No. I could have, but it would have been too humiliating. Know what I mean?"

"That must have been a real bummer, to miss out."

"The part that bummed me out," said Anne-Marie, "was that all my friends were having these graduation parties and open houses. Stuff like that. You know, where their houses get decorated with balloons and they put pictures on display from when they were a little kid."

"I'm really sorry," Crystal said.

"I wasn't a very good person, Crystal. I got suspended and stuff."

"Me too. Sometimes I would go and hang out at the mall all by myself. Just so I wouldn't have to go to school and get teased."

It sounded familiar to Anne-Marie. Not the teasing, but the part about skipping school. At least Crystal had a just cause. "People come here for all kinds of reasons, don't they?"

"That's true. All kinds of reasons. Why are you here?"

Anne-Marie hesitated. She wasn't ready to talk about the baby. "I'm trying to work out some personal problems. I need a place where I can get counsel from the Lord without a lot of outside distractions."

"Do your parents know you're here?"

"No."

"Is that the reason the problem with Michelle bothered you so much? When her parents came and forced her to leave?"

"I think so," Anne-Marie admitted. "I think that's part of it, anyway. How did you know?"

"I was talking to Jessica about it. She told me you were

real upset over it. Don't hold it against her though, she wasn't gossiping."

"There's no reason I'd hold anything against Jessica. She was just worried about me."

"Well, we're finished here, so why don't we talk to Sister Abigail about it? Here, have a look in the mirror so you can see the back."

Sister Abigail was free, so they talked to her in her quarters. Crystal began by saying that Ruth Anne was still concerned about Michelle.

"What is it that concerns you so, Sister Ruth Anne?" Abigail asked.

"I guess it was the way it was so nasty. It could happen to me. The way everyone seemed so mad and sad. I felt so bad the way they were yelling at you."

Sister Abigail shrugged. "The Lord doesn't promise us a comfy trip when we choose to follow Him, as you know. When we choose to take up the cross, it may not be made of balsa wood."

"I know, but they accused you of running a cult. Were they taking her by force?"

"They were taking her against her will, if that's what you mean. But why would anyone need to use force, Sister Ruth Anne? Do we have any bars on our windows? Are there any locks on our doors?"

It sounded as silly as it was. "No. Of course not," Anne-Marie replied.

"Do we have any gates that are closed? Any security guards? Is there any restriction on coming or going?"

"No, of course not," Anne-Marie repeated, feeling foolish.

"No one is kept at Camp Shaddai by force," Abigail reminded her. "No one is kept here against their will. Anyone can leave at any time, or call home at any time, or make any arrangements they want. There is no coercion of any kind here. Have you seen any coercion?"

"No."

"Is there anyone you'd like to call?"

"I think I need to call my sister," Anne-Marie admitted. "I promised her I would."

"Then if you made a promise, I think you ought to keep it. Do you feel like the Lord may be leading you to call her?"

"Maybe so. I'm not sure, but you're right that I need to keep the promise."

Crystal spoke up. "I'd better be going to Bible study."

"Is it okay if I stay a little longer, Sister Abigail? There's one other thing I'd like to talk about."

"Of course. Sister Crystal, please tell the group Ruth Anne will be a few minutes late."

"Okay, bye."

After she was gone, Anne-Marie summoned the courage to bring up her apprehension about Brother Jackson.

"What is it that you fear, Ruth Anne?"

Anne-Marie still relished it when Abigail and the others called her *Ruth Anne*. As a symbol of the new person she was, it gave her added confidence. But she pointed out, "It's been more than a week now. He said he'd be gone two weeks."

"Did Brother Jackson say two weeks exactly?"

"No, not exactly. He said two or three weeks." She knew she had to be truthful.

"Then can't you put your faith in what he told you? He's a man of God, is he not?"

"Oh, for sure he's a man of God. I was just hoping I'd hear from him by now."

"You know how crusades go, Ruth Anne."

"I know. Sometimes they go really well, with lots of participants and lots of conversions. When that happens, they last longer."

"Exactly. When the Lord leads, He doesn't always give us a predictable timetable or calendar. That's the beauty of His leadership."

Somehow, though, Anne-Marie felt the need to persist. "Sister Abigail, is there any way I could call him? Do you have a phone number where I could reach him?"

"I'm sorry I don't."

"Do you have an address where I could write him?" Briefly, the thought of e-mail occurred to her, but there were no computers at Camp Shaddai.

"Sorry again, Ruth Anne. The crusade he's conducting is in a rural area of Oklahoma, somewhere near Stillwater, I think. I've never been there. I don't have a mailing address."

Disappointing as this answer was, there might be a silver lining. If her parents decided to sic the cops on Brother Jackson, he would be hard to find. Very hard. If Sister Abigail didn't know how to reach him, it wasn't likely the authorities could track him, either.

Sister Abigail interrupted these reflections by saying, "I do have some good news that I can share with you."

"What good news is that?"

"Brother Jackson called here a few days ago. I talked to him."

"You did? What'd he say?"

"He told me the crusade was going extremely well, and that he still expects to return to Shaddai as soon as possible."

"When will that be?"

"Now what did we just say?"

"I know, I know. In the Lord's time, not ours."

"Amen."

Anne-Marie wondered again exactly what information Brother Jackson had shared with Abigail. *How much did she know about the relationship between Brother Jackson and herself? Did Abigail know more about his plans than she was revealing?* But that was stupid. It was worse than stupid, it was faithless. A Spirit-filled woman like Sister Abigail who kept the Lord at the center of her life would never be treacherous.

"Sister Ruth Anne, I have an observation."

"What's that?"

"I don't believe your faith is strong enough yet."

"I know." Anne-Marie hung her head.

"Don't feel ashamed. I'm not saying it as a criticism. You told me you became a Christian sometime in March when the Spirit entered you at one of Brother Jackson's tabernacle meetings."

"Yes, that's true."

"That's hardly more than three months ago. That's not a long period of time for membership in the Fellowship of believers. It takes time to make a full entry into the Spirit-filled life."

It made sense enough to reduce Anne-Marie's sense of shame. "I need more time," she said.

"You need more time, but if your efforts are sincere, the Lord will bless them. He will never turn his back on you."

"I believe that with all my heart and soul."

"I trust and pray you do. But be kind to yourself by being patient. There are so many old habits to unlearn. So many parts of the old you which need to be put aside. That doesn't happen overnight."

"I'll try, Sister Abigail. Will you pray for me?"

"Of course. I pray for you every day. I see you getting stronger and stronger in the faith. I even see you eating and sleeping better." Now she was smiling broadly. "Am I wrong?"

"No, you're right."

"Okay, then, get yourself off to Bible study. You're already ten minutes late."

Anne-Marie felt a new sense of relief. The Lord *would* lead her in all ways if her faith was unconditional. She gave Sister Abigail a big hug before she left.

That night after supper, Anne-Marie called Eleanor. She wanted to use her cell phone and call from the dorm, but she knew too many of the other girls would be there. So instead, she used the pay phone on the porch of the dining hall. No one else was there.

When she heard it ringing, she hoped Eleanor might be out, in which case all Anne-Marie would have to do would be to leave a message on her answering machine. But no such luck.

"Hello?"

Anne-Marie took a deep breath. "Eleanor, it's me."

"Anne-Marie. Baby, are you okay?"

"I have a new name here, Big Sister. They call me Ruth Anne."

"I don't care if they call you Joan of Arc. I want to know if you're okay."

"I'm fine. I couldn't be in a better place for sorting things out and seeking the Lord's guidance."

Eleanor didn't sound patient. "I called Mom and Dad like you asked me to. They were frantic, of course, assuming you'd been abducted."

"But I haven't been, see? Trust me, I'm okay."

"You can say that all you want, but I need to see you. I need to see for myself."

"Just trust me."

"No, this time I'm not going to just trust you. You're going to have to trust *me*. Mom and Dad have called me at least three times to see if I have any more information. What can I tell them? What do I know?"

"Do they have the cops looking for me?"

"I have to assume they do. They haven't said otherwise. You have to tell me where you are. I have to come see you."

"Don't ask me that," Anne-Marie pleaded. "I only called you to reassure you. Can't you tell by listening to me that I'm okay? Besides, aren't you working in that seminar?"

"I'm involved with two seminars, but they can wait. If I don't get the chance to talk to you, I can't concentrate on my work anyway."

"But we're talking right now."

"Don't play games. I mean face-to-face."

"I said don't ask me that."

"I'm asking it anyway," declared Eleanor firmly. "I'll put it to you this way: This phone has caller I.D. When you hang up, I can have the number traced. I'll call Mom and Dad and tell them where you are. They'll pick you up and bring you home. You're still underage, don't forget. Would you like that better?"

Oh God, why didn't I use the cell? Anne-Marie could feel her stomach tying itself into a knot, and it wasn't anything to do with being pregnant. She felt trapped. In her mind's eye she reviewed that horrid day when Michelle's parents came to Shaddai to drag her out. "No," she said. "I wouldn't like that better."

"Then make up your mind."

Anne-Marie sighed. Her resistance seemed depleted. She knew Eleanor didn't mean to betray her, she was just deeply concerned. "Okay, but I don't think you're like giving me a choice."

"I would think you'd be happy to see your big sister."

"Of course I would, but you have to promise to try to understand what we do here and how we let the Lord lead us."

"Right now you're the one who has to make the promises. Where are you?"

"It's in southern Illinois, but I'm not exactly sure where."

"Are you close to any big city?"

"Not that I know of. I'm pretty sure we're south of Carbondale. I guess we're not too far from St. Louis."

"Just give me the name of the place," said the impatient Eleanor. "You give me the name and I'll find it."

"Okay. It's called Camp Shaddai."

June 25

Eleanor found Camp Shaddai. Anne-Marie discovered her leaning against a blue Taurus in the parking lot by the main arch, right after Bible study. She ran to hug her sister. "You found us!" she declared.

"It wasn't that hard."

"But how did you?"

"I used a map-search program they had on the computer at the airport's customer service. That was the easy part. Finding all these back roads and knowing where to turn was a little trickier. I have to admit I had to stop and ask for directions a time or two."

Eleanor was wearing a Harvard T-shirt and blue jeans. Her hair was pulled into a casual ponytail. She looked worried, though. "Look at you. Anne-Marie, I hardly recognize you with that hairdo."

"Do you like it?"

"I guess I could learn to like it, but it's certainly different."

"It's more than a new 'do, Eleanor. It signifies the new me, the me in Christ."

"Let's don't go there right away, okay?"

"Okay." But Anne-Marie was disappointed. "You want me to show you around?"

"Later. I'm going to take you to town first."

"Town? I don't even know where town is."

"I do, though," her big sister replied. "I've already found it. Why don't you get whatever stuff you need, and we'll go to town. I think they're even having some kind of a festival."

"But I want you to meet Sister Abigail."

"I've already done that."

"You have? You're kidding, right?"

"I'm not kidding," Eleanor assured her. "I talked with her for about twenty minutes in her apartment."

"Did you ask her about taking me to town?"

"No. We didn't talk about that."

"I'll go ask her then," said Anne-Marie.

"You need permission to go to town with your sister?"

"I'm not sure. I'll go see." She ran to the dorm so she could get a little money and put on her headband. She stopped briefly in Sister Abigail's quarters to ask if it would be okay to go to town with Eleanor.

"Of course it's okay," replied the counselor. "Why wouldn't it be?"

"Okay, thanks. See you later." She gave Sister a quick hug before she left and then was on her way.

The town, Crystal Cove, was only about a twenty-mile distance, but moving along the crooked and hilly road that followed the contour of the lakeshore, it seemed much farther. It took more than forty minutes and allowed plenty of time for conversation.

"Isn't Sister Abigail beautiful?" Anne-Marie asked Eleanor.

"She is physically. I would have to wonder if that beauty extends beneath the skin, though."

"Oh no, Eleanor. She's more beautiful on the inside, even if you wouldn't think it's possible. She carries the Lord in her heart above all things."

"It sounds like you adore her, so I'm not going to speak against her."

"Adore would be too strong a word. We save our adoration for the Lord Himself. What did you two talk about?"

"We talked a little bit about the camp, why people come here, things like that."

"You didn't quarrel with her, did you?"

"I wouldn't say so. I did ask her why she hadn't called our parents to notify them where you were."

"You did? What did she say?"

"I'm sure you know the answer to that one. She said the Lord would lead you to that decision, if it was the one He wanted you to make."

"And I'm sure you thought that was a lame answer."

"I wasn't happy with it, but I didn't have a better one."

"What d'you mean?" Anne-Marie asked. It seemed like a puzzling remark.

"What I mean is, she asked me why *I* hadn't called them to let them know where you are."

Anne-Marie smiled. "I guess that was a gotcha then, wasn't it?"

"I guess it was." Then she changed the subject. "Your headband is striking. Did you make it yourself?"

"Yeah, I made it in arts and crafts. You like it?"

"I said so, didn't I? You've always been good in art."

"True," Anne-Marie admitted, "it's just too bad they have other subjects in school like economics and English and biology."

"But all your academic problems were the result of goofing off, Anne-Marie. You've always had plenty of intelligence."

"Please don't go there. I don't know how many times I've heard that from teachers and counselors. I've heard it like forever."

"I'm sorry. I guess I was trying to give you a compliment on your IQ. It didn't come out right, did it?"

But Anne-Marie was quick to reply, "It doesn't help your self-esteem to know that you're lazy, any more than you're stupid. It also doesn't help to know you have attention deficit disorder."

"I apologize again. You don't need to have low self-esteem, though. There are plenty of things you're good at." Eleanor slowed to twenty miles per hour to navigate another one of the road's sharp turns. Across the shore, the lake seemed even larger than Anne-Marie had realized. Even larger than from the perspective of Rachel's mountaintop.

"I have an older sister who's perfect," said Anne-Marie bluntly. "That tends to keep your self-esteem down."

“I’m going to tell you just how perfect I am,” Eleanor answered, “as soon as we get to town. But if you have low self-esteem, Little Sister, it can’t be my fault.”

“I know. I didn’t mean to hurt your feelings, Eleanor. I’m sorry if I did. But what is it you’re going to tell me?”

“Just . . . just be patient.”

“But what? You’ve gotta tell me.”

“I said I would, but you’ll just have to wait.”

When they got to the edge of town, Anne-Marie was surprised to discover that it was large enough to have a couple of motels and even a mini-mall with a Wal-Mart. There was a summer festival downtown, with a few carnival rides, some food booths, and an oompah band. There were face-painting booths, art exhibits, and a petting zoo.

It seemed so raucous compared to the tranquillity and serenity of Camp Shaddai. Anne-Marie wondered if that was why Eleanor had brought her here, to provide her with a renewed exposure to the “real” world.

Eleanor parked in the lot next to the L & L Motel.

“Why are you parking here?” Anne-Marie asked her.

“Because I’m staying here. I’m already checked in.”

“But I was hoping you’d stay with me. There are extra beds in our dorm.”

“Nope,” was Eleanor’s firm reply. “I’ll be staying here overnight. Tomorrow afternoon, I’ll be driving back to St. Louis. My flight to Boston leaves at four in the afternoon.”

Anne-Marie looked at the motel. It was a one-story mom-and-pop operation with doors that opened onto the parking lot. At least it looked clean. First she was disappointed that Eleanor had to come at all, now she was disappointed the two of them weren't staying together overnight. *What am I supposed to think?* "Will I get to see you tomorrow?" she asked.

"Of course. I'll drive out in the morning. That's your chance to show me around."

"Good."

It was a walk of about three blocks to the festival activities, but the streets were roped off, so there wasn't any traffic. They had hot dogs and old-fashioned funnel cakes, which reminded Anne-Marie of a time in their past. "Do you remember the time you took me with you to the state fair?"

"I remember."

"You were about eighteen. You'd just graduated high school. I was about twelve."

"I don't need help with the math, Anne-Marie."

"Very funny. I felt so grown-up and free that day, just the two of us. That was fun."

"I was in charge," Eleanor remembered. "I was the boss."

"Yeah," Anne-Marie laughed, "and you were bossy, too."

"I don't remember it that way."

"No, you probably wouldn't."

They came to a stage where southern Illinois cloggers dressed in western outfits were dancing in a line. The aluminum stage thundered like a storm beneath their cowboy boots. It was hick stuff but it seemed fun all the same.

The two sisters found a table beneath the corner of a large food tent, where they ordered Cokes. "I haven't had any junk food for weeks," said Anne-Marie. "At Shaddai, they stress health food."

"I'm glad to hear that. I guess we might as well junk it up today, then. You know those cloggers back there?"

"Yeah, what about them?"

"I don't know why, but watching them dance reminded me of that time when you and the other cheerleaders won that contest out at Centre Court at North Ridge Mall."

"That was when we were sophomores," Anne-Marie replied carelessly. "I forgot you were even there."

"I was there. I was home on spring break. I remember how impressed I was."

"You were impressed with that? All that was was stealing some dance steps from popular groups on MTV and lip-synching some of their songs."

"But it was so good. Don't you remember how the crowd loved it? I was so impressed by the way you had all your moves and timing in perfect synch."

"It was just a bunch of cheerleader moves and lip-synching," Anne-Marie repeated. "I don't know why something like that would impress you."

"I'm trying to tell you that there are things about you that I've envied."

"You envied *me?"*

"Sometimes. I envied your social skills and your looks

and your athleticism. I never could have been a cheerleader. I wasn't athletic enough, and even if I had been, the costume would've made me self-conscious."

"Oh please, Eleanor. You won the Oneppo Medal and the National Merit Scholarship and every other academic award in the whole world. Like you should be envious of *cheerleaders?*"

"You won the contest. You wowed the crowd. You took home a big trophy. Those are the facts, Anne-Marie."

Anne-Marie was so perplexed by this exchange she forgot to mention that she now preferred to go by Ruth Anne. "The trophy was a huge piece of cheap plastic," she informed her big sister. "The truth is, the figure at the top and the numbers on it broke off as soon as we tossed it in the backseat of the car. It was as phony as the whole contest."

"It may have been a cheap statue," said Eleanor.

"You won the Oneppo Medal, and you're saying I should be proud of a cheap plastic trophy we won at a cheerleaders' dance contest."

"Okay then," said Eleanor. "Let me put it to you this way." She stopped speaking long enough to rummage in her handbag until she found the box that contained the medal. She set it on the table between them. "You're so impressed with this trinket, I'm going to give it to you."

Trinket? She had to be kidding. But wasn't that the word Brother Jackson had used when he gave her the silver cross? Anne-Marie looked at the box but didn't move to open it.

"The medal's inside," Eleanor assured her. "Go ahead and check if you want."

"I believe you, why should I check? Why do you want to give it to me?"

"Because I don't want it. If you want it, I want you to have it."

"What's this about, Eleanor?"

"I'll tell you what it's about. You interrupted me a minute ago. I was about to say that as cheap as the dance trophy might have been, you won it fair and square."

"Meaning what?"

"It's what I want to tell you about the Oneppo Medal," said Eleanor. "It's what I need to tell you."

This seemed weird for sure. "Okay. What?"

"I cheated," replied Eleanor quietly. She even lowered her eyes when she spoke the words. "I won the Oneppo by cheating."

Suddenly, all the noise from cloggers and carnival rides seemed to fade deep into the background, as unobtrusive as elevator Muzak. "Cheating? What do you mean?"

"It's pretty simple. I won the Oneppo, the top of my class, even the fellowship to Harvard Law, by cheating."

"How did you cheat?" Anne-Marie found herself on the edge of her chair.

Eleanor took the time to get a cigarette from her handbag and light it up. She even offered one to Anne-Marie, who refused by saying, "No, I gave those up. It's a part of my contract with the Lord."

"I hope it's a part of your contract with your baby. If you're also eating healthy foods, I guess I need to be fair and give your Camp Shaddai some credit for that, at least."

"Thank you. What about the cheating?"

Eleanor exhaled before she said, "I was living with a man named David. We were living together in my apartment and sharing costs."

"Did you love him?"

"I wouldn't say so. We were using each other."

"Did Mom and Dad know?"

"They knew, but they weren't happy about it. That's another story. The point is, David was a computer hacker. A good one."

Anne-Marie had heard the term, but wasn't sure what a computer hacker actually did.

"The thesis I wrote which won the Oneppo Medal," Eleanor continued, "was a paradigm of a business strategy for a hypothetical company. It had to do with a personnel plan for saving significant money on health care insurance and other benefits, as well as making effective investments in current stocks."

If Eleanor was going to talk about the stock market, and use words like *paradigm,* Anne-Marie could only hope her eyes wouldn't glaze over.

"David was so good at hacking his way into databases that were supposed to be secure, that he got me inside information. For instance, he got into a database of a Wall Street corporation."

"Inside information?"

"It amounts to secret knowledge that insiders sometimes get that allows them to make lucrative investments in the market. He hacked his way in so I could use that kind of information in my thesis."

"And that's something you're not supposed to do?"

"It's something you're very much not supposed to do. It's not only unethical, it's illegal. It's even criminal, Anne-Marie."

Criminal? Anne-Marie thought. *My sister Eleanor is a criminal?*

"And there was even more. David managed, somehow, to hack his way into a government database. He got inside information on some insurance changes and loopholes that a congressional subcommittee was drafting."

"And would that be just as illegal as the other things?"

"Just as illegal, and just as criminal." Eleanor was finished with the cigarette. She dropped it into the remaining Coke and ice at the bottom of her cup.

Anne-Marie didn't know what to think. Nearly anything to do with computers was usually over her head, so she didn't understand much of what Eleanor was telling her. She didn't know whether to be disappointed in her sister or impressed that the cheating was so high-tech. It would take a genius plan to bring it off, which made it seem on a higher plane than just cheating. The only cheating she could remember doing that was remotely similar was calling in sick to the attendance office by imitating her mother's voice.

"Why did you do it?" she asked.

"I had to win because I always win. I'm always first. I always win, and I always come in first. I knew how serious the competition was, and I couldn't bear the thought of being second. Or third, or fourth. When you're used to being first all the time, you *have* to keep on winning. Second is losing. Anything but first is losing."

Anne-Marie was so amazed she was practically speechless. Finally, she asked, "Have you told Mom and Dad about it?"

"No. I haven't told anyone. Not a soul. You're the first person I've told about it."

Anne-Marie couldn't help feeling honored. "Is there any chance you'll get caught?"

"Probably not. Not at this point. Too much time has passed, and too many databases have been erased. The competition at these elite graduate schools is so cutthroat it's disgusting. You wouldn't believe the hacking, the stealing, the viruses injected into the computer systems to disable other people."

"I'm sure the Lord will forgive you for it."

"Not now, Anne-Marie; not now. The point is, I cheated for no good reason. Look at all the money our family has, and all my other academic awards. There was nothing to keep me out of Harvard Law even if I'd never even *entered* the Oneppo competition."

Anne-Marie was still stunned. She remembered Sister Abigail's words, though. "You can't be too hard on yourself, Eleanor. You were under a lot of pressure. God will forgive any sin if you make a sincere confession."

"I wasn't under any pressure except that of my own making. I'm trying to tell you that things are rarely as simple as they appear to be."

"I know that, Eleanor. The Lord teaches us to beware of the wolf in sheep's clothing. It is Satan's own strategy."

"And what about you and me, Anne-Marie? What is our own strategy?"

Anne-Marie was too confused to answer. She looked at the box on the table between them, the one with the Oneppo Medal inside.

It was as if Eleanor could read her thoughts. "So now that you know the story, do you want the medal at all?"

"Of course I want it, if you want to give it to me. I would love a gift from you."

"It's like dirty money, Baby. Now you know why I wasn't much impressed when we had that overblown reception on the lawn back home."

"But it's gorgeous, and it's from you. I don't know yet. I'm going to be praying about it, though."

Before Eleanor drove her back to Camp Shaddai, Anne-Marie stopped at the Wal-Mart to buy a small, spiral-bound notebook. She decided it was time to start keeping a journal of her thoughts and prayers. She stuck the notebook down in her handbag, right next to the Oneppo.

June 26

Anne-Marie spent a restless night. Lots of tossing and turning, trips to the toilet (for peeing, not for barfing). Eleanor, Brother Jackson, and a computer hacker named David whom she'd never met disturbed her dreams.

Her sleep was further interrupted by the restless tossing and turning of Rachel in the next bunk. She groaned and sighed. At times it sounded like pleasure, but at other times like torment.

By the time they were both awake, lying on their sides face-to-face, they had one of their whispered predawn conversations. "Can I ask you a personal question?" asked Anne-Marie.

"Why not? Do I keep secrets?"

"Why do you have troll dolls?"

"They were all gifts from my brother. Christmas or birthday gifts. I keep them to remember him by. But that's not what you want to ask me. You want to ask me about my dreams."

Rachel's perceptions were astonishing. "You dreamed the incubus, didn't you?" Anne-Marie whispered.

Rachel's eyes were wide. "I dreamed him. He took the form of a beautiful man. He tried to seduce me in my sleep."

"What kind of beautiful man?"

"A rugged, strong man with a beautiful smile and sparkling eyes. But I resisted him."

"Why? How?" Now Anne-Marie was scared.

"I had to. He wasn't who he seemed."

"How could he come to you in that form?"

"The incubus is a minion of Satan," Rachel reminded her. "He can assume any form he wants."

"Of course. If he wants to seduce young women in their sleep, why would it make sense for him to come looking really gross?"

"Exactly."

"Do you think it was a vision?"

"Maybe. It was awfully strong. I'm going to have to pray about it."

As always, Rachel's dreams and visions fascinated Anne-Marie at the same time they frightened her. "My sister is coming this morning," she said. "Can you tell me more about it later?"

"If you want, Ruth Anne. If I know any more to tell."

Eleanor arrived shortly after breakfast. Anne-Marie got permission from Sister Abigail to skip Bible study so she could show her around the grounds. After she showed Eleanor the basic everyday facilities, she took her sister to the mountaintop.

When they reached the high, high plateau where Anne-Marie and Rachel had ventured that time before, they had a spectacularly clear view far into the distance. It was a bright blue June sky with cool breezes and a few wispy cirrus clouds to highlight it.

"This is El Shaddai itself," said Anne-Marie reverently. "Exactly like the God of Abraham and all the prophets, the source of eternal strength. But don't go too near the edge," she warned Eleanor, just as Rachel had cautioned her.

They were no more than twenty feet from the edge of the drop-off to the lake. "Don't worry," said Eleanor. "I'm close enough to that edge right here where we're standing. That drop-off must be a hundred and fifty feet, at least."

"I've only been here once before," said Anne-Marie. "But it's where I felt the closest ever to Almighty God. It was as if the Lord was seated right here beside me. Rachel, too. We came here together."

Eleanor took a kerchief from her pocket to wipe some of the sweat which had gathered on her forehead. "Let me bring you face-to-face with some facts I'm not sure you ever thought about," she said to Anne-Marie.

"What facts?"

The big sister pointed. "Look across as far as you can to the other side of the reservoir. That could be six or eight miles from here."

"I know. Isn't it beautiful?"

"Incredibly beautiful. Abraham had a god on his mountain, but other distant mountains and valleys had their own gods. Some of them had goddesses, as a matter of fact."

"Yes, but they were false gods."

"Beyond that far place, we know from experience, is the town of Crystal Cove. If we were standing here thousands of years ago, they'd have had a god of their own, too, most likely."

"But it would only be another false one. The Bible is full of misled people who worshiped false gods and graven images." She wondered where Eleanor was heading with this line of discussion.

"Floods came," Eleanor continued. "Droughts came. People died and the crops stopped growing. Wars were won and lost. Ancient people used such signs as proof that some gods were stronger than others. They often absorbed gods into their cultures if they thought they were more powerful ones."

"Yes, but El Shaddai is the one true God and Father of us all. What are you getting at?"

"I'm telling you you haven't studied enough history. Most religions make gods they like and then keep them that way. Unless they find a way to make them better, like borrowing someone else's. They don't like to believe that God is unknowable. Something beyond what we can imagine."

"But we don't have to imagine. God speaks to us through His Word. We have His Word that He sent His only son to dwell among us and give His life so that we could be saved. And I don't know why you're cutting me down like this. Do you think it will help somehow?"

"I'm not cutting you down, but I think somebody needs to talk tough with you. I talked tough with myself yesterday. I confessed something to you that no one else knows, and for which I feel a lot of guilt and shame."

"But I told you the Lord will forgive your sin. Take it to Him and all you have to do is lay it at His throne."

"Yes, you did tell me that. But I'm more interested in achieving my own forgiveness. It was a treacherous thing I did, but I did it of my own free will. I want you to come to your senses now."

"You think I'm in a cult, don't you?" Anne-Marie accused.

"I think you're very close to it," replied the older sister. "But I'm not sure exactly how to define what a cult is. You received good counsel at the Planned Parenthood clinic, and an invitation to follow up with another appointment. You turned your back on it."

"I'm sure that Nurse Howard meant well, but she has limitations because she doesn't dwell in the Spirit. Besides, I found out that they perform abortions after they lure you into a false sense of security."

Eleanor's tone of voice revealed her diminishing patience. "Do you remember anything in our conversation with that nurse that seemed misleading or tricky?"

"No, but that's what makes it so good and clever."

"Come on, let's start back down. I can't leave any later than noon."

They made their way along the path, stopping to lean against a huge boulder along the way, which made time and space for Eleanor's final agenda. "Brother Jackson is the father of your child, isn't he?"

Anne-Marie was caught off guard. "What makes you think so?"

"I don't know, I just believe he is. You tell me."

"I'm pretty sure he is, yes." Anne-Marie's answer was equivocal because she remembered her conversation with Sister Abigail about dreams and desires.

"*Pretty* sure?"

"Yes, that's what I said. *Mostly* sure."

"Mostly sure. Anne-Marie, I want a straight answer before I leave. When are you going back home?"

"I can't say right now. I'm just waiting on the Lord to lead me."

"And Brother Jackson? Are you waiting on him as well?"

"Yes. That too. When he comes back it will help me all the more."

They started walking again. Anne-Marie was in the lead while Eleanor conversed from behind: "When did he say he'd be coming back?"

"In two weeks," Anne-Marie answered quickly, without turning around. She quickened her pace.

"And it's been over two weeks. What does that tell you?"

"It tells me his crusade in Oklahoma is going better than expected. That's how it happens when you let the Lord direct all your ways. When it's time, he'll be back."

By the time they reached the small footbridge where Rachel had done her tightrope act, they paused again to rest. *And behold, a pale horse.* Anne-Marie remembered how disturbed she'd been that day.

"I'm going to be just as tough on you as I was on myself yesterday," Eleanor declared. "The reality is that he's probably not coming back at all."

"Don't say that. You can't say that."

"There's not even a reason to believe he's actually in Oklahoma. He could be any place, even out of the country. He has to know that he might be a fugitive from the law, so he ought to be smart enough to squirrel himself away where he can't be found."

"You don't know him!" Anne-Marie exclaimed. "You've never even met him!"

"The next thing you'll be telling me is that I don't have enough faith. Well let me tell you something: I have plenty of faith in my own brain and my own resources, which is the kind of faith I think *you* need to develop."

"I'm telling you Brother Jackson is a man of the Spirit. Why can't you listen to me? The Lord leads him in all things."

"You said that before. I'm telling you I don't think he's coming back at all because he can't be that stupid."

"I don't know why you're even talking to me like this! I don't even know why I told you where I was."

"I would never do anything to hurt you, at least not on purpose. You know that. I wouldn't have come all the way here at the expense and inconvenience if I didn't love you and want to help you."

Anne-Marie knew that was true. Even though she was bewildered and frightened, she did feel certain of her sister's love and affection. But at this moment it seemed irrelevant.

The sisters were on the move again, heading back in the direction of the complex. "I've got one other thing I have to say," said Eleanor quietly.

"What?" asked Anne-Marie, knowing she didn't want to hear it.

"I'm giving this one week. One more week and then I'm calling Mom and Dad to tell them where you are."

"You wouldn't."

"I would and I will. It tears me up inside to stall them when I have real information. Today is the twenty-sixth. I won't await any longer than July third. When I call them, I expect they'll be here to get you immediately."

"I can't believe you would be that mean."

"You mean you can't believe I would be so determined. Well, believe it. I won't be able to take it any longer."

Anne-Marie started to cry. "Just go back to Boston," she sobbed. "Go back home and cheat on some more projects."

June 27

Eleanor went back to Boston. What she left behind, though, was an urgency which tormented Anne-Marie. The one thing she couldn't stand was the thought of her parents showing up here and taking her home—the humiliation would be too great. She wrote feverishly in her notebook: *Eleanor is wrong in saying Brother Jackson won't return. He will return, but in his own time, as the Lord leads him.*

My time is short though. Eleanor said one week, and today is the twenty-seventh.

The most devastating thing, the one thing I could never bear, would be if my parents came to Camp Shaddai to take me away.

And then she added, *Somehow I have to forgive Eleanor. The Lord would want me to.*

There was a small library in a room just off the cafeteria. It had books in two bookcases, and all members of the group were free to study there for meditation and reflection. In addition to the many volumes of God's Holy Word, there were dozens of inspirational Christian books to help guide in Spirit-filled living.

There were also a few books on demonology, to help the reader understand the nature of Satan's treacheries. Early in the morning, Anne-Marie looked up the incubus in one of the books, and discovered him to be what Rachel had described: a demon who could change form as he pleased and seduce young women in their sleep. He could even impregnate them during the visit.

An incubus, according to the literature she browsed, could even take female form and seduce a sleeping male. The female form was called a succubus, though. But that was unusual. The most common condition was for an incubus to appear in the form of a sublime male, to provide a woman with a much better lover than any mere mortal could ever be.

Anne-Marie thought of Brother Jackson immediately. She opened and closed the book absentmindedly, repeating to herself the words *a sublime male . . . a far better lover than any mere mortal could ever be.*

She started her fast right after breakfast, which consisted only of some orange juice and some weak tea. She had actually learned to like the beverage in small doses, but only if it wasn't brewed strong and had sugar.

At the conclusion of morning Bible study, Anne-Marie asked the group to join her in a prayer of forgiveness. She asked God to forgive her for the way she'd spoken to Eleanor when they parted. She beseeched Him to understand it was just her spur-of-the-moment anger, that she knew deep in her heart Eleanor was only trying to help, to the best of her ability.

"She can only follow what light she's given," said Sister Abigail. "You are right to seek forgiveness."

It prompted Anne-Marie to pray that Eleanor would discover the inner light of Spirit-filled living so she could understand those things which seemed so far-fetched to her. While Anne-Marie offered up this prayer with sincere fervor, Crystal squeezed her hand tightly on one side, and Jessica on the other.

It brought a certain relief but only briefly. While the others began leaving for chores, Anne-Marie kept her seat. "Are you coming, Ruth Anne?" Sister Abigail asked her.

"I'd like to stay and pray for a while, if it's okay. I'll catch up my chores later?"

"Of course. I couldn't help but notice you didn't eat much breakfast. You're not losing your appetite again, are you?"

"No, my appetite's just fine. I promised the Lord I'd fast, though."

"For how long?"

"I think maybe two or three days. My time is growing short."

"If you feel that way I'm sorry, but what about the Lord's time? How short is His time growing?" Abigail asked the question with a patient smile of affection.

"I don't know. That's one of the things I have to pray about."

"Fasting can be beneficial, but do be careful. If you're fasting for two, please be twice as careful." Her smile seemed to grow bigger.

"Have you ever fasted, Sister Abigail?"

"A time or two, I have. That's why I say it can be beneficial. It can purify our systems, which can make us more open to the Lord's guidance."

"That's what I'm hoping."

"Just remember to be careful. Let me know how it's going."

"Okay, Sister. God bless you."

"And God bless you, Ruth Anne."

As soon as Sister left, Anne-Marie took out her notebook again. She started by writing Eleanor a letter, apologizing for the nasty things she'd said and asking forgiveness. It wasn't a long letter, and it wasn't hard to write, particularly since she'd confessed her sin and asked forgiveness.

The harder things to write were the notes she'd started making to herself on another page. They were pressing, soul-searching reflections prompted by Eleanor's visit.

Abortion is murder. The Lord could never forgive it, so I can't consider it.

I need to speak to Brother Jackson about all of this. A baby has a father, not just a mother. His thoughts will be very important.

I feel certain that Brother Jackson is the father. I'm pretty convinced about that part.

Anne-Marie ran out of thoughts so she stopped writing. She took out a tissue to blow her nose and while doing so, felt the lump in her pocket. It was the Oneppo Medal. She took it out to look at it. The wind blew the trees around, so she had frequent glimpses of the silver lake. She held the medal up against the light and turned it around slowly.

In this light, with the lake providing the background, everything but the obelisk seemed to vanish. It seemed to exist in the air, suspended magically. It was stone and hard. When Eleanor had argued with her about religion, she'd mentioned that in very ancient times, stones were gods. They were worshiped. Like evergreen trees, they were adored because they seemed immortal—unchanging.

Then this Oneppo Medal was not only a symbol of Eleanor's dishonesty—it was also like a pagan idol, the kind of stone altar worshiped by idolaters condemned in the Bible.

But she couldn't just throw it away. She put it down. As soon as she began writing again, her thoughts turned to disturbing, darker elements:

Rachel dreams the incubus, but that doesn't necessarily mean it's a vision. Even she says so herself.

It doesn't mean the incubus is a vision having anything to do with me. Just because I'm sleeping in the closest bunk, she could share it with anybody.

Rachel's dreams of death on the footbridge are in the same category. They aren't necessarily visions, and they aren't necessarily intended for me.

Then she thought to add, with a knot forming in her stomach, *If you were seduced by the incubus, you would be impregnated by the demon seed. You would be carrying the devil's own offspring, maybe even the Antichrist.*

She had to pause for some deep breathing. She chewed at the eraser before boldly writing her final observation, and this time all in caps:

MY BABY IS BROTHER JACKSON'S, NOT THE INCUBUS'S. I JUST KNOW IT, KNOW IT, KNOW IT!

It was just before lunch when she saw his car. There was the old rattletrap Chrysler, parked beside three other, newer cars.

Anne-Marie stopped in her tracks long enough to make sure her eyes weren't playing tricks on her. No! It *was* his car!

Brother Jackson was back!

With a mixture of joy and apprehension, Anne-Marie ran in search of him. She didn't find him in the cafeteria, or the administration building, or in any of the small shelters they used for tabernacle meetings and Bible study.

After she checked the dorm, she made her way rapidly to Sister Abigail's quarters. Brother Jackson wasn't there, either, but Abigail was.

"He's back!" Anne-Marie declared breathlessly.

She was smiling. "Are you surprised, Ruth Anne?"

"No. I don't think so."

"Good. When we wait upon the Lord, He will fulfill His promises."

"Do you know where he is? Do you know where I can find him?"

"I'm not sure where he is at this moment. But you'll see him soon. He plans to stay for a few days."

Anne-Marie thought, *I was right to put my trust in the Lord. Eleanor was wrong. She might have meant well, the words she said may have been sincere. But she was wrong as she could be.*

"I'm going to keep looking for a while," said Anne-Marie. By this time, she had recovered most of her breath.

"Fine, but don't be late for lunch."

"I'm fasting. Don't you remember?"

"No," said Sister Abigail, "I guess I had forgotten that. But you can drink fruit juice and be at the table with us for fellowship."

"I had fruit juice for breakfast."

"You can drink water, then. But please join us."

"For sure."

When she left, Anne-Marie wondered where she might look next. She might follow the path into the woods and look down along the small footbridge. But then she thought of the shed where they kept the maintenance equipment, and the adjacent shop. She remembered Brother Jackson's fondness for tractors and other mechanical things.

And that was where she found him. He looked about the same, except his hair was a little longer. He was wearing a pair of faded blue jeans and a white T-shirt with words which read: LIFE IS SHORT. PRAY HARD.

It was a disappointment that she found him talking to Jessica, besides two of the maintenance men. It was like a social gathering, so being alone with him wouldn't work. He greeted her warmly, with a firm hug, and smiled that beatific smile.

"How are you?" he asked her.

"I'm fine," she lied. The timing wasn't right for talking about the inner fears and indecisions which gripped her.

He held her at arm's length so he could look her over. He had a firm hold on both of her shoulders. "I understand you are now Ruth Anne," he remarked.

"Yes I am."

"A new woman, reborn in the company of the Lord's fellowship. I hope and pray that Camp Shaddai has been helping to light your way."

"I wait upon the Lord and put my trust in Him," said Anne-Marie.

"Praise Him."

Then Jessica joined them. She said, "Brother Jackson and I go way back. I was at two of his crusades in southern Wisconsin. Once last year and another time the year before."

"It's always a joy when we can fellowship together again," said Brother, giving Jessica a squeeze on the shoulder. "I brought Sister Ruth Anne here from up in Indiana," he told Jessica. "She needed a place for undisturbed peace and reflection."

"I know." Jessica smiled at Anne-Marie. "Ruth Anne is sincere in all her efforts. We all like her."

Anne-Marie appreciated the compliment, but she wanted Brother Jackson all to herself at this moment. She felt ashamed at her own petty jealousy. A man of God would of course make time for every member of the flock.

"Tell us about the crusade in Oklahoma," said Jessica. "How did it go?"

"Better than expected, praise God," was Brother Jackson's reply. "Hundreds of souls were brought to Christ, many of them for the very first time. The crowds were so large we had to extend the mission by a couple of days."

"Praise Him, then," said Jessica.

"Praise Him," added Anne-Marie.

Then Brother Jackson turned to talk to the mechanics again, and unworthy as Anne-Marie's disappointment might have been, she seemed helpless against it. *He didn't even notice my hair. He didn't even say anything about my hair.*

That evening, Sister Abigail made an announcement in the shelter. She told the group that Brother Jackson had agreed to lead them in fellowship. He delivered a spirited message on the Rapture and its true meaning.

"The Lord is coming again, and He is coming soon," declared Brother. "The signs are all around us in a culture which is obsessed with filth and degradation. He will not be patient with the wages of sin. He is coming again and He is coming soon. It could even be tomorrow or the next day; we never know.

"What we do know is that His coming will be a trumpet call to glory and a chorus of the heavenly host for those who have kept His company and lived according to His Word.

Those who have taken up His cross, who have fellowshipped in the Spirit, will be lifted up to join Him in the air to live in eternal glory. Those who have chosen to live the secular life of greed and wantonness will be left behind. For them, the future will be a desperate and eternal suffering."

Those who have kept His company will join the Lord in the air, Anne-Marie repeated to herself.

"Those in His company, those who have waited upon His guidance to submit and to serve, those have no need for any fear of death. They will never die because the Lord will lift them up to be with Him in glory for all eternity."

Some of his subsequent words were lost on Anne-Marie because she reflected joyfully on this one eternal reality which surpassed all others: If she waited upon the Lord and served Him always, she would be lifted up, and the lifting up would be for always. She thought of the mountaintop. If the Rapture was coming, that was where she'd want to be. There was nothing to fear. *Nothing.*

At the close of the fellowship, when they joined hands and lifted up fervent prayers, there was much speaking in tongues around the circle. Even Anne-Marie herself found an inner river of transcendent hope and anticipation which took the form of little sobs and groans.

She slept soundly that night, undisturbed and at peace.

The next morning, refreshed but a little on the lethargic side, she sat through Bible study in a passive mode. She was distracted. She reminded herself if she was shaky or passive, the fast she was on was probably to blame. But it was going to have a consequence of a different kind of nourishment: purification.

She wondered when she would have a chance to speak to Brother Jackson alone. But the calming effect came when she remembered that waiting upon the Lord's time had brought him back to Camp Shaddai.

At the conclusion of Bible study, she stayed behind again to write in her notebook.

Eleanor was wrong about Brother Jackson. I put my faith in the right place.

Thinking of Eleanor reminded her of the Oneppo Medal, which reminded her of the cheating. But the medal itself might represent idolatry, mightn't it? Which would be a whole lot more sinister than simple academic cheating.

She shook her head and looked for concentration. She wrote: *I would love to be alone with him, but I can't be petty. Jealousy would be petty and worldly. We are all one in Christ, so Brother serves the whole community of fellowshippers, not just me.*

Today is the twenty-eighth. I have five days left.

This last observation ignited a new wave of panic, but it didn't last long. The fasting seemed to be producing the mellowing effect she'd hoped it would. Everything seemed to be moving more slowly. She felt receptive. And if the Lord was coming soon so she could join Him in the air, there was nothing to fear. Not Eleanor, not her parents, not the deadline or contract at school. Not diplomas. Not even Satan himself.

From her seat in the shelter, she watched the two figures in the distance, moving slowly along the wooded path in the direction of her favorite footbridge. One of the figures was Brother Jackson, and Rachel was the other. Her head was lowered, and Brother had his arm around her shoulders as if to comfort her. They walked slowly, but they were too far distant for Anne-Marie to tell if Rachel was in tears.

Her curiosity got the best of her. *Are they talking about me? Are they talking about one of Rachel's visions and how it might affect me?* She followed them, keeping a safe distance. She couldn't have done otherwise, in fact, because of her decreased physical energy. Moving slowly, she came to a mossy boulder. She sat down on it. She could see them sitting on the footbridge, but she was still too far away to tell what they might be saying. It was obvious from Rachel's body language, though, that she was sharing inner and private elements with him.

Anne-Marie watched. Brother squeezed Rachel's shoulder at one point while he pointed to the heavens with his free hand. His smile gleamed as brightly as the sunlight that struck the surface of the water.

He took the form of a beautiful man, thought Anne-Marie. Those were the words Rachel had used that morning a few days earlier to describe the form in which the incubus appeared to her. *He took the form of a beautiful man.*

That wasn't all Rachel had said, though. She'd added something else. Anne-Marie searched her memory, but the words didn't come back to her until she looked again at Brother Jackson. He was still gesturing passionately while guarding Rachel with his strong arm around her shoulders. *A rugged, strong man with a beautiful smile and sparkling eyes.*

He took the form of a beautiful man. A rugged, strong man with a beautiful smile and sparkling eyes.

Anne-Marie felt increasingly drowsy. In spite of her keen interest in the exchange between Rachel and Brother, she got out the notebook again so she could write:

If the demon can take any form it wants, it can appear in the form of Brother Jackson.

But if my life is service and submission, fellowshipping with the Lord all my days, I will never die. There is nothing I need to fear. The Rapture is coming soon—the Lord is coming again, and I will be lifted up to join him in the air.

That evening, Brother Jackson shared with the group the highlights of the conversation he'd had with Rachel on the bridge. "Sister Rachel is blessed with the gift of prophecy. The Spirit has bestowed the gift, but she is young in the fellowship. She doesn't always understand the meaning of her visions."

Rachel told the group that Brother Jackson was revealing her inner prayers with her permission; he wasn't betraying a confidence.

"We prayed about it," Brother continued. "We asked the

Lord's help and His guidance. Her Spirit-filled gifts are bountiful, but she is still a child. The longer she lives within the life of the Spirit, the more understanding will come her way. When that happens, she will join the gift of interpretation with her gift of prophecy."

"Yes," many of the group responded. "Praise for the wisdom."

"All praise."

"Until then," Brother Jackson continued, "her gift will not necessarily comfort her or bring her fulfillment. It may bring confusion and fear, as it often does. Am I right in saying so, Rachel?"

Rachel nodded. "That's exactly it."

"What we all need to learn from this," explained Brother Jackson, "is that the bestowing of gifts of the Spirit is not always a source of comfort or inner peace. Part of it can seem nearly a torment. But even so, we have no reason to fear. Our future is eternity with the Heavenly Father; we have His Word on it.

"If a gift of the Spirit seems a burden sometimes, it is one which the Lord wants us to carry. No one ever said that to pick up the cross and follow Him would be easy. You already know that from your own experience. Those who follow Him unconditionally are frequently cast out, ridiculed, and even persecuted."

"Yes, it's true," Anne-Marie murmured. She felt lightheaded.

Brother Jackson concluded his remarks: "If you find

yourself blessed by gifts of the Spirit, don't let them frighten you. Instead, wait upon the Lord to help you understand. He wouldn't give you entry to the Mysteries, then leave you to fend for yourself. 'Wait patiently upon the Lord,' His Word tells us. Unlike other burdens, sacrifices in service to the Lord are joyful because they are opportunities to submit and to serve. Submitting and serving bring you into the flock of the Chosen. And never forget the glorious redemption, remember the Rapture, which may be coming much sooner than we might expect."

June 29

When she finally got to meet with Brother Jackson alone, it wasn't alone at all. It was in the company of Sister Abigail, in her quarters. She had the tea poured ahead of time.

Anne-Marie might have been annoyed or discouraged that Sister had to be with them, but she was too lethargic. Two and a half days of fasting, subsisting exclusively on fruit juice and water, left her drained.

Brother Jackson took note of the silver cross he'd given her, still secured to the ring at her navel. Embarrassed, Anne-Marie tried to pull her shirt down far enough to cover her midriff. "It's a beautiful cross," she said, speaking slowly. "It will always be special to me."

"It's what resides beneath the cross that troubles Ruth Anne's soul," observed Sister Abigail. "She is carrying a child. She prays over the dilemma daily and seeks the Lord's guidance. She's even been fasting to make herself more receptive to His wisdom."

"I remember," said Brother Jackson. "It's why I brought her here in the first place. Is the Spirit leading you here, Ruth Anne?"

She felt light in the head, so her answer was slow in coming. When Brother Jackson turned to face her, he seemed to turn in slow motion, then turn again several times in rapid succession, like some of those optical tricks she could remember from MTV videos. She thought of her sister. She thought of the counselor at Planned Parenthood. She thought of Rachel's vision of the incubus, and how the demon could take the form of a beautiful man. She thought of the dreams she'd had of Brother Jackson, and the way they'd stimulated her. When she finally answered, she said, "I believe the Lord will light my way."

"Have you received encouragement yet?" he asked her.

"Yes," she answered firmly. "My sister said you wouldn't come back, but now you have. I was right to put my faith in the Lord."

"Praise Him," said Brother Jackson.

Sister Abigail said, "All praise." Then she added delicately, "Ruth Anne was once under the impression that you are the father of her child."

"Mmm," murmured Brother Jackson, arching his eyebrows.

Anne-Marie watched the arching brow, but it was like the MTV thing; the eyebrows seemed to lift again and again.

"She shared a dream with me," said Abigail, "in which you came to her as a lover. We talked about it for a while, and of course we prayed about it."

"Of course."

"The dream was so real to her, she wondered if it wasn't in fact a thing which actually happened."

"A young woman this beautiful," Brother Jackson interjected, "would make it hard on me or any other man. It would be the Devil's own temptation, and that's a fact."

"We talked about Satan's possible role in her dream experience," Sister Abigail continued, "and how He would seek to disrupt her spiritual search by any means possible. Am I getting this right, Ruth Anne? Is this an accurate summary of our conversation?"

The words were exactly right. "Yes," answered Anne-Marie. She couldn't help gazing at Brother Jackson. He was *the beautiful man.* The lassitude which consumed her left her to simply look and listen.

"Rachel dreams the incubus," said Anne-Marie. "He comes to her in the form of a vision."

"Have you discussed this with her?" asked Sister.

"Oh yes, several times. Do you think her vision is intended for me?"

Abigail smiled sweetly. "Unfortunately, I've never been blessed with the gift of interpretation," she said. "I have to be honest and admit my own limitations."

Brother Jackson added, "Rachel is blessed with gifts of the Spirit, but don't forget what I said last night. She is young and often uncertain about interpreting her own visions."

Even in her listless condition, Anne-Marie knew how right he was. Rachel had told her that the time she envisioned her mother's death, she didn't actually know that was the specific meaning of the prophecy. At least not until after her mother was dead.

"I wish I could give you a certain answer to your questions," said Abigail gently. "I have prayed about it fervently, I can assure you."

"We have prayed about it together," added Brother Jackson.

"Eventually, the answer will have to come from the Lord Himself, and no other way," said Abigail.

Anne-Marie knew they were right.

"You look sleepy, dear. Do you need to take a nap?"

"Maybe after Bible study," Anne-Marie replied.

"Are you sure the fasting is something which is going to benefit you?" Brother Jackson wanted to know. "Maybe the time has come to get some food inside you."

"Maybe," she answered. "But I need to keep the fast at least for the rest of today."

It wasn't until after lunch and crafts that she found herself alone with Rachel. Anne-Marie was in the laundry room of the dorm, ironing her headband. She was using the tip of the iron to work on the wrinkles, being careful all the time not to scorch the letters. She didn't have much experience at ironing, and to try it on delicate fabric with close detail work was a challenge. Twice, fatigued, she sat down to rest.

"Are you okay?" Rachel asked her.

"I'm light in the head sometimes," Anne-Marie admitted. She was still recalling the conversation with Brother Jackson and Sister Abigail. It was amazing how things that seemed so simple could turn out to be so complicated. But then, why should she expect the world of the Spirit to be simple?

"Are you still on the fast?" Rachel asked.

"Yeah, I'm still on."

"Maybe you should get something to eat. Start another fast another time." Rachel started folding towels.

"Not today. My promise to the Lord was that I would keep the fast for three days. Maybe tomorrow I'll have some fruit." She got up to iron a little more, but then sat down again within two or three minutes.

"Rachel," Anne-Marie asked, "when you dreamed the incubus and it was the beautiful man?"

"Mmm?"

"Was it Brother Jackson? Was it Brother Jackson's form the incubus took?"

"Don't ask me that."

"But I need to know. It's the one thing I have to know."

"But you just can't ask me that. Not that question."

The one question I can't ask? Anne-Marie tipped her head back. "But I have to know. If your vision was meant for me, I have to know."

"Please don't ask me that. I'm not even totally sure it was a vision." Rachel began folding the towels more aggressively, but to Anne-Marie, in her spent condition, she seemed to move in slow-motion stages. That MTV thing again.

"But I have to. Can't you see? I just have to." She felt almost too weak to argue, but her urgency was so intense. "Did the incubus take Brother Jackson's form in the dream?"

"Do I have to answer that, Ruth Anne? Can't you just let it go?"

"No. I can't let it go. I'm begging you to tell me."

"Begging?"

"Yes, begging. I *have* to know."

Rachel kept her eyes on the towels. "Okay yes," she said. Her voice was scarcely more than a whisper.

"What about me?"

"What about you?"

"You know what I mean: Was I in the dream, too?"

"Okay yes," admitted Rachel, turning her back. Once again, her voice was very quiet.

Rachel dreamed about the pale horse and the footbridge. The Scripture passage was bold in Anne-Marie's mind: *And I saw, and behold, a pale horse, and its rider's name was Death, and Hades followed him.* "How was I in it?" she demanded. "How?"

"You were just in it. Your face was. It was a scrambled dream, the hardest kind to interpret." Rachel turned to face her. She put a hand on her hip. "Okay, yes. I dreamed the incubus and the pale horse."

"And me, too. I was in it, too."

"Yes."

"Is this what you and Brother Jackson were talking about on the footbridge yesterday?" asked Anne-Marie.

"Yes, that was most of it. If it was a vision, it was one that scared me."

"It's scaring me, too."

"You see?" said Rachel. "You see why I didn't want to answer your questions? I can only hope the Lord will forgive me."

"But why do you need forgiveness, Rachel? You're only sharing your gift."

"Because I'm scaring you and I don't know how to interpret the vision. It puts me on shaky ground."

Anne-Marie was so tired she felt nearly exhausted. But she had to press on. "And did Brother Jackson know how to interpret the vision?"

"No. He urged me to wait for the Lord's guidance."

"The bridge with the pale horse means death," said Anne-Marie slowly. "The incubus appeared in the form of the beautiful man. What if I'm carrying the seed of the demon?"

"It may not mean that at all. That's only one possibility."

"Yes, but what if? Does it mean I should like kill myself to kill the demon seed?"

"Of course the Lord doesn't want you to kill yourself."

"How do you know that?"

"Because suicide would be just as big a sin as abortion. Now can we drop this? I feel terrible because I've scared you. I wish I hadn't let you drag it all out of me."

"But your gift can only help me, Rachel." *Could I inter-*

pret the dream myself? Anne-Marie wondered. *The pale horse and the incubus and me? Is it possible the Lord is giving me the gift of interpretation?*

She asked Rachel that question: "Do you think the Lord would bless me with the gift of interpretation?"

"Praise God if he does, but you can only wait and see."

Then Anne-Marie thought of the Rapture. She remembered the radiant smile on Brother Jackson's face from two nights before. Joining the Lord in the air for everlasting, holy bliss. "Do you think the Rapture could happen for one person?" Anne-Marie asked. "You know, like the Lord lifts us up as individuals after we have entered His Kingdom here on earth?"

Rachel took Anne-Marie by the shoulders. Her grip was tight. It hurt. "That would be a miracle," she said. "Now we need to drop this subject. At least I do." Her dark eyes were suddenly wild, flecked with green particles. She let go of Anne-Marie's shoulders. She was still moving in slow motion.

Now Anne-Marie was exhausted. She said, "Miracles are not so unusual. The Lord blesses people with miracles all the time."

"You're scaring me, Ruth Anne."

"I don't mean to," Anne-Marie replied. The idea of death frightened her; she was not nearly strong enough to overcome the fear of it. "The Lord blesses people with miracles all the time," she repeated. "There are miracles all throughout the Bible. Brother Jackson even had one on an oil rig. It changed his life."

Rachel said, "Remember how you said that sometimes I scared you? Well it's the other way around now. You're scaring me. You've got to remember that I don't always know what my dreams might mean. Like the dream I had about my mother and the angels. I didn't know it was a vision until after she died. I told you that, remember?"

"I guess you did. I'm not sure what I remember right now." Luckily, she remembered to unplug the iron. The headband was neatly pressed. "I think I need to go and take a nap," she said.

"I wish you would. And I wish you'd start eating again."

"Tomorrow I will. But I promised the Lord a three-day fast." Walking slowly, she headed for her bed.

June 30

This was her time. She heard the Lord's call and she would answer.

She had to move carefully in the dark to avoid colliding with a bed frame or one of the hutches. Noise was out of the question because it would probably awaken someone, and this needed to be a private moment. It needed to be *supremely* private.

In fact, she moved more cautiously than the situation demanded. The steady hum from the window fans created a blanket of sound that would muffle any bump or stumble. Because she was so shaky from the fasting, though, she watched her steps with extra care.

There was enough light for maneuvering in the dark from the outside pole lamp, once her eyes got adjusted. She wasn't sure what time it was, since she had been dozing in fits and starts. It was probably two or three A.M. Her belly was tight and acidic. The concrete floor was very cool on the soles of her feet; it felt good.

When she left the dorm, she was careful not to let the screen door slam.

Ruth Anne was headed for the mountaintop.

She was walking along the dark path in the direction of the footbridge, but the moon was full. She could navigate her way. She passed one of the shelters where evening testimony was held, as well as crafts and Bible study. It seemed so strange to see no faces, hear no voices. It was more than silence, it was *hush*. She took it as an underscore for her current spiritual mindset. It wasn't long before she could see light at the rear end of the footbridge, peeking among the dense foliage.

She was wearing her white Jesus shirt and her overalls. She had on clean underwear, because it seemed important to be presentable in the unlikely event they ever found her body. As a matter of fact, during the several hours or so since she had made her final decision to take her burden up to El Shaddai, the question of clothing had been a distraction: *What will you look like if they find your body?*

But it was more or less irrelevant, because if her own death was indeed her final answer, she wouldn't really be taking her own life, she would be flying to the Lord. That would be her personal miracle, to join Him in the air. Even dying would not be death in any conventional sense. She would be gone, but she would be in loving arms where no one left on earth could ever see her. The Apostles' Creed said the "resurrection of the body," not just the soul.

There was a chance she would be vanishing without a trace. The Lord would lift her up on His own terms. When there was triumph over death, death was not a factor. If they did find her in the gorge, they wouldn't find a corpse; they would find a glorified body rather than one of earthly substance. Nothing anyone could touch or experience like flesh—even if the corpse was still *in* the world, she herself would no longer be *of* the world.

She was scared. Very scared. But just as determined. Damp and clammy clay formed the pathway. At another time, under different circumstances, the sharp pebbles which gouged her feet would have been painful. But now, navigating her way in the dark, weakened and woozy, it was all she could do to concentrate on watching her step. Under other conditions, she might have smelled the petroleum odor of the weather-treated footbridge.

As she approached the bridge, nausea bubbled in her chest. She belched some viscous vomit into her mouth, swallowed, and then there was that bitter, metallic aftertaste like that of a penny resting on her tongue. It was fear that caused her to quicken her pace, but as soon as she did, she found herself so fatigued she needed to stop and rest against the railing. *Whatever happens to me up on the high mountain shouldn't be fearful, since I'm simply answering the Lord's summons. "If God is for me, who can be against me?" . . . "Whither thou goest, I will go. . . ."*

She rested her head on her forearms for a few moments,

waiting to recover her strength. She heard an owl hooting in the cottonwoods. They had owls here, and they had hawks. But no Canada geese. She hadn't seen a single goose since she'd been here. This was the bridge that was the setting for Rachel's recurrent vision of death. In so short a time, it had already become a bridge filled with memories.

At first, listening to Rachel's vision and trying to imagine how it might apply to her, Anne-Marie had thought of abortion. Even though the Lord hated abortion, and so did she, it might be different if she were carrying the demon seed. In the demon seed was the Antichrist. If Brother Jackson wasn't really the father, if the incubus had visited her in her sleep and impregnated her, it might be the one exception which could make abortion acceptable in the sight of God.

But then she'd pondered that perhaps the vision of death was more probably intended for her than for her fetus. If she took her own life, she would take the demon seed with her. Suicide was a sin and might jeopardize her place in the Lord's mansion, but maybe the circumstances that consumed her would, again, be acceptable in the sight of God.

But still: What death? In whose service? What kind? In what sphere? How glorified? Anne-Marie recognized her reeling questions for what they were: panic. It was her mission now to trust in the Lord and pray that those who might be left behind would be able to do the same.

She spoke out loud for the first time: "But why do I presume death at all? Of any kind? My most fervent prayer is that on the mountaintop the Lord will give me an emphatic and bold answer to my prayer for understanding. I'll have closure. I can move forward in the Fellowship without lingering doubts."

If she did die, she knew that Sister Abigail would understand and would even use her death somehow to exalt the Lord. It was obedience. It was faith. *And death shall have no dominion.*

She moved with care along the planks, fingering the crude handrail gingerly as she went. She didn't want any splinters in her hand. On the far side of the bridge, standing beneath the other feeble pole light, she stopped long enough for a few deep breaths. It was time to put the headband on before she went a step farther. She tied it neatly and deliberately; the two strands of excess ribbon hung limp at the back of her neck, except when the breeze fluttered them.

The nausea she felt wasn't the same as the nausea of morning sickness; this was nerves. But the trembling of her limbs was something different altogether. It was more than panic, it was panic intensified by three days without food. *If my will is strong enough, though. If my will to serve and obey is just strong enough. . . .*

It was a long, draining climb up the steep and rocky path that led to the plateau of mountaintop, to the sacred height of Rachel's El Shaddai. It was dark most of the way. She was feeling her way, not seeing, but she had traveled this path before. She had to stop and rest frequently. Fortunately, there were those familiar boulders she could sit on until she was ready for more climbing.

She began her slow climb again, a few feet at a time between stops. In the clearings, the full moon helped to light the way. It had to be a sign that the Lord wanted her here. He wanted her here and now, in this place.

By the time she reached the top, she was utterly exhausted and light-headed. The rocky shelf of plateau was well-lighted by the moon. With no hesitation she made her way directly to the edge, sat down firmly, and let her feet dangle. The strong light from the moon enabled her to see clear to the bottom, even though the precipice upon which she perched herself was so very high above the shoreline. The reservoir was low from lack of rain, so the shoreline itself was a shelf of rocks and sand. Her feet were swinging freely back and forth.

She sat without trepidation for several minutes, long enough to regain a sense of equilibrium. She made her heart wide open before she said, "Dear Jesus, Dear Lord Jesus," out loud. She sought the words that would make the perfect prayer, so as to encourage the Lord to deliver her an unequivocal sign. Her wide-open heart was ready to submit. Even death couldn't be scary, because to know the answer would overcome any fear. But she couldn't find the right words, in spite of her best intentions.

But how much would the words actually matter if the Lord knew the purity of her heart? *Was it death? Was it incubus?* The affairs of the Spirit were so elusive, but God would lead.

She sat alone with the Lord, in the dark, at the top of El Shaddai.

The Lord had led her here. It wasn't likely that she would fall; instead, the Lord would lift her up. She expected her own private Rapture; her own personal miracle. She believed in it with all her heart and soul.

In her escalating drowsiness, she didn't notice that she was leaning forward precariously. Her mind wandered to Rachel's supreme reluctance to share the meaning of her dream. *I wish I had the gift of interpretation, but the Lord hasn't blessed me with it.* She remembered Brother Jackson's advice to *put all faith in Him and He will light your way.* Well, there was light here for sure.

She gazed at the beauty of the moon path where it streaked the surface of the lake. It was hypnotic. The water was so still, the path of moonlight was as unwavering as a royal carpet. The water carpet itself might be the sign, or at the very least the setting for the sign. The Word said that the Lord had walked on water.

It would happen there, she felt certain. Could it be that the gleam on the water was the runway where the Lord would make himself visible to her? And would He appear all in white, cloaked in a resplendent pure gown of a special heavenly substance? And reach out His eternal arms so that she might step off the cliff to join Him in the air? And if so, there would be no body ever found, no corpse, only her glorified absence without a residue or a trace. Was this the way the Lord would bring closure and glory?

But an hour of openness, of submission, and receptivity, and she didn't hear an answer. Didn't see one, either. It might have been longer than an hour, perhaps even two; her sense of time was as out of joint as her other senses. She watched and waited a little longer, but then fell asleep, on her side.

When she awoke, just before dawn, she sat up slowly and rubbed her eyes. She felt keen discouragement combined with acute fatigue and drowsiness. The Lord's answer had not come to her in spite of her climb to this sacred place.

In His time, not our time, wasn't that what Sister Abigail always said? Wasn't that what Brother Jackson preached as well? *In His time* was what true submission was all about. She couldn't let her disappointment weaken her faith.

She thought of her sister Eleanor's impatient ultimatum, but held no animosity. Eleanor cheated to win the Oneppo Medal. Had Anne-Marie thought to bring her diary notebook, she might have written this information on a page all its own. She thought of Nurse Howard, back at that clinic, who had shown her a pamphlet about parenting.

She thought of her parents and the contemptible contract that had taken away her freedom and dignity. If she ever had any dignity to begin with. But haggard and spent as she was, lacking sleep and food, even the thought of her parents coming to take her home was all of a sudden not threatening anymore. Ruth Anne was empty.

Still discouraged but weary and maybe even wiser, she stood up to leave. It had seemed so certain that the time for her sign was now. It was still dark, so at least she could return to the dorm without waking people. She would tell Rachel about this, but no one else.

This morning I'll have fruit. But she stood up much too quickly. Her head swam and her limbs tremored so that she nearly blacked out. There was nothing to reach out for or lean against.

She lost her balance.

In the instant before she fell, she thought of her parents, her sister, and finally of Brother Jackson. She didn't think thoughts, she simply watched the faces racing through her mind's eye.

Then she was free-falling. The panic tore at her insides as she searched for perfect prayer words one more time. It took less than two full seconds before the rocky shore came up to savage her. She died without regaining consciousness.

A later coroner's inquest would reveal that had she fallen during a wet season, when the water level would have been higher, she might have survived.

Epilogue

"'He who believeth in me,'" began the minister, reading from a series of Biblical passages, "'though he were dead, yet shall he live.'" The minister was a Presbyterian clergyman, the pastor of the church in which Anne-Marie Morgan had been raised. He was a thin, pale man who wore a clerical collar. But his voice was rich and resonant.

"'Let not your hearts be troubled,'" he continued, "'but believe in God and believe also in me. In my Father's house are many rooms; if it were not so, would I have told you that I go to prepare a place for you? And when I go and prepare a place for you, I will come again and will take you to myself, that where I am you may be also.'"

The graveside service was a simple, brief one, limited to family and closest friends seated on folding chairs beneath a canopy. The canopy wasn't really necessary because the weather was fine, but it provided a sense of additional privacy. Security personnel had cordoned off a section of the cemetery. There were curious onlookers and even a Minicam or two, because of the controversial nature of the circumstances of Anne-Marie's death as reported in some of the articles in the local papers.

The minister closed his Bible before clasping it firmly with both hands against his stomach. "Anne-Marie Morgan," he began, "fell to her death in a camp in southern Illinois. We gather here to celebrate her life, to grieve for our collective loss, and to take comfort from the fact that she dwells now with the Heavenly Father."

Then he began quoting Scripture without reopening the book. "'If I speak in the tongues of men and of angels, but have not love, I am a noisy gong or a clanging cymbal. And if I have prophetic powers, and understand all mysteries and all knowledge, and if I have all faith, so as to remove mountains, but have not love, I am nothing.'"

At this point, Eleanor, who was seated on one of the folding chairs between her mother and her Aunt Grace from Cleveland, took steadfastly from her purse Anne-Marie's handcrafted headband with EL SHADDAI in the vivid white letters. Slowly but carefully, she tied it around her head so that it was secured straight and firm above her long ponytail. Cheerleader hair.

Her appearance couldn't have been any more incongruous. She wore a simple, black sleeveless dress which was quietly elegant. She wore a string of pearls. And now, a ribbon headband.

The minister seemed nonplussed. Whether he was distracted by Eleanor's simple, dramatic gesture, or whether he wished to reinforce the poignancy of the Scripture, it was hard to tell. Nevertheless, he paraphrased the passage from First Corinthians. "If I have the powers of prophecy and tongues, and understand all mysteries, but have not love," he said, "I am nothing. I am a noisy gong or a clanging cymbal."

When he was finished with his remarks, which took no longer than ten or fifteen minutes, he quietly shook the hand of each family member and whispered his condolences. Eleanor, her father, and her mother each tossed a white lily on top of the silver casket.

Her parents then headed for their car, her father's arm around her mother's heaving shoulders. Eleanor left them briefly to make her way across the lumpy terrain in the direction of a blue Topaz parked beneath a large oak tree.

The car belonged to Sister Abigail, who was standing against the front door, her arms folded across her chest. It wasn't easy for Eleanor to traverse the cemetery lawn, not in her high heels. She took them off. When she neared the car, Sister Abigail said, "May the Lord bless you with His peace."

"Thank you," said Eleanor curtly.

"I felt compelled to come," said Abigail, "even if just to watch from a distance."

"You know," said Eleanor, "I don't think I've ever slapped anybody's face before." She didn't raise her voice, but she must have had a tone, because Abigail flinched.

"I see you're wearing her headband," said Abigail quickly. "I can't think of a better way to honor Ruth Anne's memory."

"There never was a Ruth Anne. That was just some sort of mystery fiction to satisfy your religious agenda."

"I would never quarrel with you at a time like this. The Lord would surely disapprove."

"*Disapprove* would be the word," Eleanor confirmed. "I'm not wearing my sister's headband to honor her memory. I'm wearing it to remind me of my own shortcomings and the humility I need to learn."

"The Lord blesses us for humility."

"Then He must bless us for learning something from it. I didn't have the resourcefulness to give Anne-Marie the help she needed, and I certainly didn't have the courage. I could have forced her to go back home, where she could have received the full spectrum of counseling and options. I didn't do that. I didn't have the spine. Neither did you."

"We put all our trust in the Lord," answered Abigail quietly, "receiving direction from Him in His time, not our own."

"That will be your excuse then. I won't have one. And the headband will remind me of it. I'm not nearly as good as I think I am. I have to get back to my parents now. Good-bye."

"Just a minute, please," said Abigail. She reached in her purse and produced an object which she offered to Eleanor. It was the Oneppo Medal.

Eleanor held it in the hollow of her hand while Sister Abigail explained, "It wasn't with her other things. We found it in one of the shelters near the creek. I wanted to return it to you."

Eleanor stared at the medal until her tears started to flow. "Thank you," she finally said as she turned to go.

She made a U-turn, though, before she headed for the car to join her parents. She carried her pumps in her left hand. She approached the grave where the lilies still lay on the casket. Some workers were beginning to dismantle the canopy. Eleanor came to within ten feet of the open grave.

She was no athlete, but she gave the Oneppo an underhand, arcing lob. It sparkled in the light like the gem that it was, or might have been. Her aim was accurate. The medal landed cleanly in the open grave without even striking the casket.